When will Serena free herself to love again?

"You have a wonderfully warm, embracing nature, Serena Van Buren," he declared softly, the deep, vibrating sound of his voice striking a chord of excitement in her heart. He took her hand in a gentle grip, but she still refused to meet his gaze. "When do you plan to start living your life again?"

Serena closed her eyes briefly. "I'm living my life."

"Through others, maybe, but not for yourself. Every patient you see receives a healthy dose of your compassion and understanding, but you have needs, too." He raised his other hand and traced the outline of her face with his fingers.

She shivered and pulled away. "Don't you do the same thing? It's been five years for you, and you haven't remarried." Her voice sounded shaky and unsure to her own ears.

His hand fell away, and the white gleam of his teeth revealed his sense of humor. "At least I'm making an effort to join the ranks of the living again. You're not helping me."

HANNAH ALEXANDER is the pen name for a husband and wife multi-published writing team from Missouri. Melvin Hodde works as a doctor while Cheryl writes full-time. They are very active in their local church and mission projects.

Books by Hannah Alexander

HEARTSONG PRESENTS
HP274—The Healing Promise
HP337—Ozark Sunrise

A Living Soul

Hannah Alexander

Heartsong Presents

We wish to thank Sharon Heidlage, who first gave us the idea for *A Living Soul* years ago when she worked as a counselor in a place like Alternative. Thank you to Lorene Cook, whose attention to detail and encouragement has helped improve this story. Thank you to Mary Young for helping us with ideas for the cover. Also, thank you, Rebecca Germany and Cathy Hake, for your valuable input. God bless you all!

A note from the author:
I love to hear from my readers! You may correspond with me by writing:

Hannah Alexander
Author Relations
PO Box 719
Uhrichsville, OH 44683

ISBN 1-58660-148-2

A LIVING SOUL

Cover illustration by Lisa Peruchini

one

The baby would die if Mother had anything to do with it. Kirby knew that. Mother hadn't changed in two years, hadn't even known what her own daughter was going through. This time she would know, but it would be too late. Kirby placed her hand over her abdomen and tried to feel some emotion, but she couldn't. It was just as well. Emotions got her into trouble.

She bent over the blank piece of paper and sucked on the end of her ink pen. What did one write in a suicide note? "Dear Mother and Father," she mouthed the words slowly as she wrote, then frowned and almost crossed them out. Why not call them Mr. and Mrs. Acuff? That was how she thought of them now. She felt so separate from them, so different. So alone.

A noise reached her from the other room, and she tensed. A knock. The doorbell chimed through the house, and she held her breath. It was Jenny, of course. Good-girl Jenny, who went to church, read her Bible, talked to God every day whether she needed to or not. They were supposed to go to the movies tonight with some of their friends.

"Sorry, Jenny, not tonight," she whispered, then waited until the noise stopped before she continued with the note. "I'm taking Dad's old junker on a drive tonight," she wrote. "I'm sure you'll see it again. . .you just may not see me."

She reread the note and grimaced. It sounded like she was running away. Of course, they would know soon enough what had happened. But it still needed more. "I can't live with my past. Can you?" There, that would make them stop and think.

The small handful of tiny white pills in the pocket of her

blue jeans would take care of everything. What good was her life, anyway? She was a pain to her parents. She was disposable. All the guys felt that way. Use and dump. The instructions must be written on her forehead in letters that flashed on and off when she met a guy she liked. She thought Kyle would be different, but as soon as she told him she thought she might be pregnant, he ran off like she'd sprouted an extra head.

She had already cost her parents more money for a counselor than she was worth. That was why they'd terminated treatment. They'd stopped church a long time ago, only a couple of months after they started taking her. If they thought the religious goodness of those people would rub off on her, they would soon be disappointed—even though that was where she met Jenny. And that was how Carson Tanner came into their lives.

Kirby lay the note on the kitchen table, bent down to tie her hiking boots, and grabbed a bottle of juice from the fridge—had to have something to wash down the pills. Had to have a flashlight, too. . . . There would be one in the car.

❧

Misty dusk gradually cooled the hot, muggy August evening as the mauve beauty of a Missouri sky battled for attention against the lush foliage of Jefferson City. Hungry nighthawks dipped and plunged within the reflected lights from the street.

Serena Van Buren lay on her back on a blue-gray Berber carpet, absently staring at the sunset through the plate glass window of her family room. Her thoughts drifted with the haunting bird cries that echoed through the growing darkness.

Tossing her head to chase a stray tendril of short, silver-blond hair from her cheek, she stretched her legs out in front of her and glanced up at her mother-in-law, who stood by the window, arms folded across her stomach, fingers tapping in silent contemplation.

"I still miss him, Blythe."

Their golden cocker spaniel pup, lying curled up in a corner of the sofa, caught the caressing softness in Serena's voice. He raised his head and looked at her. She was lost once more in her contemplation of the sky when the animal stretched, leaped from the sofa, and boldly walked over to nuzzle her face. She absently raised a hand to keep his pink tongue from her lips.

Blythe turned and glared at the pup. "Rascal, get back." He turned a sorrowful gaze up at her, drooped, and slunk back to the sofa.

Blythe smoothed her gardening tee shirt down over her jeans. "Of course you miss him. You always will. But you can't just bury yourself with a dead husband." She sank into the overstuffed easy chair and swung her legs up beside her. "And don't start telling me about loyalty, either. Jennings was my own son, and I miss him, too." She hesitated, cleared her throat. "You're thirty-seven, Serena. It's time to be getting on with your life."

Serena stretched and yawned to hide an irrepressible grin. Blythe had preached this sermon before. "Yes, and you sure set a good example, didn't you, Pal? How many men did you go out with after Papa died?"

Blythe glanced away. "That's nonsense. I was a good twenty years older than you are when I was widowed."

"And still as active and beautiful as you were at thirty," Serena retorted.

"If you think I was beautiful at thirty, you haven't looked at our picture albums."

"Don't give me that, and don't change the subject. Life doesn't end just because you've had your sixty-seventh birthday, you know. If you wanted male companionship, you could have it, so don't preach to me about growing stale."

Blythe spread her arms. "Look at me. Who'd want an old raisin like this? It's just not the same."

Serena flashed her a warning look.

"Okay, okay." Blythe waved a hand casually. "All I'm saying is that a woman like you shouldn't finish her life alone. You're too young. It's been three years."

"I'm not alone."

"I don't mean the girls. You know the kind of companion I'm talking about." Blythe narrowed her eyes.

Serena chuckled. "Would you stop—"

The front door opened suddenly, then slammed as angry-sounding footsteps echoed along the hallway. Serena's older daughter, Jennifer, came striding into the room, her pretty, oval face flushed, her golden brown eyes flashing fire.

"Jenny?" Serena straightened. "Honey, what are you doing home so early? I thought you were going to eat after the movie."

Jennifer strode forward and flopped down onto the sofa, her long, brown hair tumbling across her shoulders in a loose cascade. "How can guys be such. . .such insensitive jerks?"

"Another fight with Danny?" Serena asked.

"Yeah, but Mom, it isn't just him. I'm worried about Kirby?"

"Kirby Acuff? What did she do?"

"It's what she didn't do that worries me. She was supposed to go with us to the movies tonight, but when we went by to pick her up, she wasn't there. At least, she didn't answer the door. And she never showed up at the movies, so afterward I wanted to go back to her house and check on her, but the guys didn't want to waste the time." The grim set of her jaw line expressed her displeasure with her other friends.

She reached into the pocket of her white shorts and pulled out a ring. She held it out in the palm of her hand to show Serena. "This is why I am so worried."

Serena stared at the ring, a beautiful, glowing opal set in gold filigree.

"Mom, this was Kirby's prized possession. Her favorite uncle gave this to her on her fifteenth birthday. She came by the clinic today when I was painting the hallway, and she just gave it to me. She seemed really down."

Serena studied Jenny's face with growing concern. "Did she say why?"

"Just that she wouldn't need it, and she knew I always admired it."

"And she was supposed to go to the movies with you and your friends?"

"Maybe she went somewhere with her parents." Jenny shook her head, worry growing more evident in her expression. "I don't know. Her boyfriend broke up with her a couple of days ago, and I know that hurt her bad. Mom, in psych class last year we learned that when someone was thinking about suicide, one of the things they did was give their stuff away. Like this ring. I don't want anything to happen to her!"

"And Kirby's seemed depressed lately? Has she talked about killing herself? Has she given other things away?" Serena pulled herself up from the floor and sat on the sofa next to her daughter. "Honey, I trust your judgment. Do you think Kirby is in the frame of mind to do something like this?"

"I don't know. . .I think so. I hate to accuse her of. . .but Mom, we can't take any chances, can we?"

Serena picked up the telephone on the end table beside the sofa. "What's her number?"

Jenny gave it to her, and she dialed and waited. Almost before the first ring ended, someone snatched it up. "Hello, Kirby? Is that you?" came a man's frantic voice.

"No, Mr. Acuff, I'm sorry," Serena said. "This is Jenny Van Buren's mother, Serena. I think we've met at some school functions a few times."

There was a disappointed pause. "Oh. Dr. Van Buren."

"Please call me Serena. I'm sorry to bother you like this,

but Jenny and I are worried about Kirby. Obviously, she isn't there, and she was supposed to go out with Jenny and some friends tonight. She gave—"

There was a sudden shuffling at the other end of the line, and Serena heard a woman's voice raised in anger—or in alarm—in the background.

"Hello?" Serena said.

"I'm. . .sorry, Serena. We can't find her. She left a note on the kitchen table telling us she took my old car, and she hinted that we may not see. . .see her again. I'm not sure. . .I don't know what to think."

Serena's concern deepened to alarm. "Is there any luggage missing? Are her clothes gone? What about shoes? Any indication that she might have run away, or—"

"Her overnight case is in the hall closet, and Carol says Kirby's hiking boots are gone."

"Hiking boots?" Serena echoed.

"Yes, but she wears them all the time."

"Mom." Jenny lay a hand on her arm, her brown eyes widening. "Kirby loves the Katy Trail. She goes hiking there a lot, and she's always trying to get me to go with her."

Serena covered the mouthpiece of the phone and murmured to Jenny, "But it's nighttime."

There was a cry of surprise over the telephone, and Serena heard Kirby's mother shout in the background, ". . .missing! They're gone!"

"Oh, no," Mr. Acuff moaned. "Look, Serena, I've got to hang up now. We've got to call the police. Carol's sleeping pills are missing." There was a click, a silence, then a dial tone.

"What, Mom?" Jenny asked, grasping Serena's shoulder. "What happened?"

Serena replaced the receiver and turned to her frightened daughter. "Honey, Kirby's mother is missing her sleeping pills."

For a moment, Jenny's fear reflected across her face, spiraling out of control. And then, as if by conscious effort, she pressed her lips together and took a deep breath. "Okay, Mom. We've got to help look."

"Yes, we do. Give me a list of some of her favorite places, because if she's planning to end her life, she may want to surround herself with those things she loves the most."

"I already told you, Mom. The Katy Trail. She loves that place. She's always trying to get me to go hiking with her."

"Which trailhead?" The Katy Trail was a railroad track converted into a hiking trail, and it stretched across the countryside north of Jefferson City.

"It's where the trail goes through Hartsburg. You have to drive up Highway 63 eleven miles, then turn left. There's a sign."

Serena stood and Blythe did the same. "I'll get my shoes on, and then I'll take the van and drive there. Jenny, you stay here on the phone and call more people. See if you can convince your friends Kirby could be in real trouble. Blythe, take your car and start checking the parks. She may have decided not to go all the way out to the trail, but I can't imagine she'd want to be around any crowds."

"I'll call Carson Tanner, Mom. He'll go. He's always trying to get Kirby to come to church."

Carson. Yes. The thought of him helped calm Serena's swiftly increasing stress level. "That's a wonderful idea, Honey. Call Carson. He can help us search." She grabbed her cell phone, jammed on her shoes, and raced out to the garage.

two

The old Ford was parked in the gravel parking area, and it was empty. Signs beside a small bathroom pointed both directions along the smooth trail, now swallowed in the darkness of night. All Serena had was her small flashlight, which didn't have the illumination she would have liked. But the car was here. Kirby had to be nearby.

She flipped open her cell phone and punched her home number. Jenny answered immediately. "Honey, the car's here, right where you told me it would be."

"Oh, Mom, did you find Kirby?"

"Not yet, but you need to call the Acuffs and tell them, and they'll need to alert the police. Did you reach Carson Tanner?"

"Yes, he's on his way out there." Jenny's voice wobbled, and Serena heard the tears in her voice. "I hope she's safe. I hope she hasn't. . ."

"I know, me, too. Which direction does she usually go? East or west?"

"She always goes west. She says she's always wanted to head the direction of Kansas and never stop walking."

"Okay. I'll be in touch." Serena said good-bye and hung up. The dusty white trail crossed through the tiny village of Hartsburg, and elderly homes hovered in the darkness. No one seemed to be out, and Serena decided not to waste time trying to find someone to help her search. She crossed an old railroad bridge and entered a deep passage of forest. "Kirby!" she called. "Kirby, are you there?"

No answer. No telling how far she might have gotten by now.

Serena first met Kirby Acuff about two years ago when

Jenny brought her home from church one Sunday afternoon. Since then, the girls had become good friends and remained so even after Kirby and her parents stopped going to church. Jenny had lamented several times how sorry she was that Kirby had no Christian influence at home and didn't always make the best decisions. Tonight's decision could be the worst—and last—of her life.

"Kirby!" Serena called again, farther down the trail. Still no answer. Time to pick up the speed a little more.

Not only had Jenny introduced Serena to Kirby, she had also introduced her to Carson Tanner, the church youth leader, who worked as an ER physician at St. Mary's. As Serena was an OB/Gyn affiliated with St. Mary's, they had a lot in common. They had become good friends, taking lunch breaks together whenever possible—although, with their work schedules, that wasn't always a dependable thing. Their rapport had grown, but when her daughters and Blythe began to invite him to family dinners, Serena realized what was happening. She ended the relationship. She couldn't take it further; she wouldn't do that to a man again.

Under Carson's direction, the church youth group had doubled in size over the past two years. At least, that was the information Serena received from her family. She, herself, had not attended since Jennings died three years ago. That was her biggest source of conflict with her children and Blythe. It frustrated her, and it hurt them, but she didn't know how to fix it.

"Kirby!" she called again. Still no answer, but she thought she heard a skittering of footsteps and a rattle of rocks. "Kirby, is that you? Please talk to me. Your family's worried about you. Jenny's frantic."

A whisper of sound. . .a sniffle, a soft moan. Serena rushed forward, shining her light back and forth across the trail. "Honey? Kirb—" She saw a patch of white, a fall of blond hair, to the left of the trail in the shadows. Serena stepped toward the girl in the darkness and felt the brush of a branch from an overhanging tree ruffle her hair. "Kirby, it's me. Serena Van Buren." She aimed her flashlight off to the side a bit so the girl wouldn't be blinded by the beam. "You have a lot of people worried about you."

Kirby shook her head, pursing her lips defiantly. She did not reply, but tears filled her eyes and dripped down her face. All this Serena saw in the glow of her flashlight as she stepped closer.

"I know about the note you left your parents," Serena said softly. "I want you to tell me if you're planning to hurt yourself."

Kirby dashed at the tears with the back of her hand, smudging thick mascara. "Leave me alone."

Serena stepped in front of her. "No, I can't do that."

Kirby glanced over her shoulder along the blackness of the tree-shrouded trail, as if she might bolt in that direction.

Serena reached out and touched the girl on the shoulder. "Have you taken your mother's pills?"

Kirby didn't look at her.

"I'm not joking here." Serena's voice grew firmer, more insistent.

Kirby glanced into her eyes, then looked away quickly. "No."

"Walk with me, Kirby. Come on. Use your flashlight and keep an eye out for the snakes," she commanded with the same quiet authority she sometimes used with her daughters.

Like Serena's daughters, Kirby resisted for a moment, then turned and fell into step beside Serena. They walked a few yards in silence, toward the village, with only the echo of their footsteps to disturb the peace.

"Talking won't help this time, Serena," she stated sullenly, her voice hoarse with tears. "I'm not playing games."

Serena's worry grew. This talkative seventeen-year-old was

unnaturally quiet—for Kirby. "Have you already done something to hurt yourself? Have you—"

"No, I haven't done anything, okay?" Kirby snapped. "I didn't expect to be hunted down like some wild animal!"

"You haven't been 'hunted down.' " Serena retained her "mother" tone. "You have friends and family who love you and want to make sure you're safe."

"Oh, sure." Sarcasm drifted heavily through the darkness. "Mother and Father wish I'd never been born."

"Difficulties with your parents can always be worked out. Jenny's worried. Do you mind if I call her on my cell phone to let her know you're safe?"

Kirby shook her head. "Go ahead," she said softly. "I didn't want to worry her."

Serena did so quickly, and when Kirby refused to talk to Jenny, Serena said good-bye and disconnected. Then she turned back to Kirby. "Tell me, why did you give your ring to Jenny? And where are your mother's sleeping pills? I've spoken with your father. The police are looking for you."

Kirby jerked to a stop, and her eyes flew open wide. "What! They called the police! What are they going to do, arrest me for grand theft auto?"

"Don't change the subject," Serena said. "They're afraid you're going to commit suicide."

Kirby's firm pointed chin wobbled, and her eyes filled with fresh tears. She turned and strolled along the trail again. Serena followed, and waited, and wished she had the right to pray. This girl desperately needed prayer—and she needed to be talking to someone who had a good relationship with God right now. Serena did not.

"What else did my parents tell you?" Kirby asked at last. "For instance, did they tell you how we played God with an innocent life?" There was a deep bitterness in her voice and a tone of intimate revelation. She had decided to talk.

"For instance?"

"Babies," Kirby mumbled. She wiped her eyes, streaking more mascara across her face.

Serena's throat tightened. She swallowed hard. This girl's pain radiated through the warm summer night like a mist.

Kirby took a deep breath. "I never told you, did I?" She stared hard at Serena, shaking her head slowly. "I never told Jenny." She walked along in silence for a long moment, sniffing, wiping her face with the back of her hand. "I had an abortion two years ago, when I was fifteen."

Serena felt the shock of Kirby's words all the way through her body, and she instinctively felt her pain. It took a moment to recover her equilibrium and voice. "You could have told me, Honey. How I wish you had. I could have helped you. There are counselors—"

"We tried a counselor. Obviously, it didn't work."

Serena searched the agonized young face. "What do you mean?"

Kirby closed her eyes. "I'm pregnant again," she whispered. "And you know what? The guy who's the father broke up with me. Just dumped me flat."

Serena felt a lump forming in her throat. "I know it hurts, that it's frightening. I understand."

Kirby shook her head. "You can't know how it feels. Nobody can know what this is like unless they've been through it already and know they're going to have to do it again. Especially when. . .I can't help wondering if Mother would have gotten rid of me the same way if. . ."

"But she didn't," Serena countered softly. "And you're not alone." She stopped and reached out to the young woman. "Kirby, look at me." She waited until the tear-washed eyes slowly came open. "A lot of young women have felt the same self-hatred you're feeling."

"You think so?" Kirby's voice was filled with sarcasm. "You haven't talked to many girls my age lately."

"Yes, I have. Don't forget I run Alternative. I'm sure Jenny's told you about our free clinic. I talk to a lot of young women there and in my practice. Many don't struggle with it, I know, but many others do. They realize. . .they know. Kirby, I'll be here for you." She paused. "Are you sure you're pregnant?"

"I took a home preg test," Kirby said. "The last time, I was in the last part of my second trimester when I had the abortion. I even felt. . .felt kicking before Mom guessed I was pregnant and took me to the doctor. When my parents find out, they'll make me—"

"No." Serena's hands tightened instinctively with sudden outrage at the Acuffs. What had they done to their daughter? "They can't force you to have an abortion. No one can do that."

"You don't know my mother. She's like a rhinoceros on a rampage."

Serena studied Kirby's expression through the dim light. "Is she. . .abusive?"

"She doesn't hit me, if that's what you mean. She yells a lot. She's just. . .you'd have to see her to know what I mean."

Serena stopped walking and touched Kirby's arm. "Come see us at Alternative. We provide emotional support and even housing for unwed mothers. If you need someplace to stay—" Should she be saying this? Was she trying to alienate Kirby from her own parents? But what they were doing. . .was trying to take a baby's life. "And we can find good homes for the babies."

Kirby watched her for a moment. "I guess I never thought about going there myself."

"Why not? It's a clinic for young women just like you, who are lost and frightened, but don't want to terminate a pregnancy."

Hope flickered in Kirby's expression. "You'd really help me? Even if my parents—"

From the distance, a deep, male voice reached them. "Hello. . .Serena? Kirby? Are you out there?"

Serena called back, and as she did so, she felt Kirby tense beside her. "It's okay, Honey, it's Carson Tanner. Jenny called him about you."

Kirby caught her breath. "What did they do, call the whole city?" Still, there was a hint of relief in her shaking voice. Carson had a special way about him that appealed to teenagers —and not just teenagers, but people, in general. Patients trusted him. Staff worked well with him.

"I know he's kept in touch with your family," Serena said. "He cares very much about you. Do you think you could confide in him about the pregnancy? He's not going to judge, and I know he'll want to help you as much as possible."

Kirby hesitated, and a residue of tears sparkled in the glow of their flashlights. "But what if the test is wrong? Maybe—"

"At Alternative, we can give you a pregnancy blood test, and you and your parents can get counseling and help."

"But I don't want to tell my parents about this. You don't know my mother. She'll make life miserable for everyone if I don't do what she wants me to do."

"Aren't your parents friends with Carson?"

Kirby nodded. "Kind of. After I had my first abortion, they got desperate. They took me to a psychologist. That was a downer for me, so they went really nuts and broke down and went to church—you know, where Jenny and Emily go. We attended for a couple of months. Carson visited our house several times, and I know my parents liked him. He's even been to see them a few times since we quit. He doesn't harass us or anything, he just listens. My parents don't have a whole lot of friends. Mother doesn't get along with a lot of people, but I think she likes Carson."

"Why did they stop going to church?" Serena knew everyone had their reasons. She had her own.

"Mother said she got tired of hearing the preacher talk about sin and salvation all the time. He really blew it the day he preached on abortion. Mom freaked. That was it for them. I kept going with Jenny for awhile, though, until Mom decided they might corrupt me." Kirby snorted in contempt. "Right. Like I'm corruptible."

Serena placed her arm around the teenager's shoulders. "My dear, I realize you don't have a very high opinion of yourself right now, but I think you're someone very special."

There was a surprised pause. "You do?"

"Yes. Let's hurry and meet Carson."

There was barely a second of hesitation, then, "I guess. . .I could talk to Carson about it." After another minute she cleared her throat and said softly, "So you. . .you know. . .you think I'm okay?"

"Very okay." Serena gave her a squeeze. "I've known you ever since Jenny brought you home that first time, and I love your sense of humor, your kindness to Jenny's younger sister, Emily Ann, and your interest in their grandmother's garden."

"Yeah, sure. You make me sound like a saint."

"No, I'm telling the truth. You're obviously desperate to prevent another abortion, and you obviously didn't want the first one, but killing yourself and your baby is not the way to change things. Two wrongs don't make a right. Two deaths don't make a life."

Kirby was thoughtfully quiet a few more yards, then said, "I couldn't do it, Serena. I wouldn't really be able to hurt my parents that way. I just don't—"

"Hello!" Carson Tanner stepped out of the gloom along the trail.

Kirby jumped, startled, and aimed her flashlight at him. He wore cut-off blue jeans and a white tee shirt. His short, black hair was spiked up in the back, as if he might have been sleeping before the telephone call woke him up. He looked tired. Those night shifts in ER could take it out of a person.

"Kirby, praise God, Serena's found you!" he exclaimed as he rushed forward and caught Kirby in a quick, enveloping hug. When he looked at Serena over Kirby's head, she could see the relief and joy in his eyes.

He released her and stood back. "Young lady, have you—"

"No, and you can cool it with the inquisition," Kirby said, focusing closely on his face, as if watching for his emotional reaction. "Serena's already said it all. No, I haven't taken any pills, no I'm not going to hurt myself. . .and I don't want another abortion." Her eyes narrowed.

Serena held her breath as she, too, watched for Carson's reaction.

There was only a slight pause and no change in his expression. He held her gaze. "Sounds like we have some talking to do, my friends."

ªª

Carson knew he couldn't let the shock show in his expression or in his voice. He'd worked with plenty of troubled teenagers, and he knew the games they sometimes played to get past an adult's defenses. He kept his voice deep and calm.

He was glad Serena had been the one to find Kirby. People couldn't help being drawn to Serena's compassion, and he was one of those people. Her obvious inner convictions reflected in everything she did, in spite of the fact that she seemed to have an emotional block against anything that had to do with God. Since she'd been very active in church before her husband's death, he couldn't help wondering if she was still angry with God for taking Jennings at such a young age.

Kirby touched his arm as the three of them walked toward the trailhead. "Carson, Serena and I have been talking, and I want you to help me tell my parents if I'm pregnant again."

"Of course I will," he said, feeling his stomach clench in protest. Kirby's parents could be on the difficult side—or at least Carol could be. Hal pretty much fell in line with whatever his wife wanted. But whatever they were like, Carson wouldn't allow Kirby to face this alone. He knew Serena wouldn't, either. "Are you sure that you're pregnant? Have you had a test?"

"Serena said I could go down tomorrow to Alternative and have one, but I don't want to talk to them about it tonight, anyway. Please don't tell them yet."

"They'll most certainly want to know why you're so upset tonight. It's my understanding that they've called the police, and they may very well show up here in the next few minutes."

Kirby rubbed her eyes wearily. "I just can't face it all tonight."

Hal and Carol Acuff were arriving at the trailhead as Carson emerged with Kirby and Serena.

Carol, a slender, frazzled woman with tightly curled blond hair, rushed ahead of her husband in the glow of their car's headlights. "Kirby! Baby, what you put us through!" She reached out to hug her daughter, but Kirby shrugged from the embrace.

Serena saw the darkening of pain in Carol's eyes as she lowered her arms to her side. "Why, Baby? Why did you do this?"

Hal stepped forward with tears in his eyes and wrapped his arm around Kirby's shoulders. "We're so glad you're safe. You don't know how scared we were." He turned to Carson, and lines of worry seemed etched more deeply around his eyes than the last time Carson had spoken with him. "Thanks so much for coming out here." He nodded toward Serena, then reached forward and shook her hand.

Kirby darted a suddenly nervous gaze around the parking area. "Are the police coming?"

"No, we called them and told them we'd found you." Carol

held out her hand. "Where are they?"

Kirby's eyes widened, and she blinked at her mother. "What do you mean?"

There was a waiting silence while mother and daughter attempted to stare each other down. Kirby broke the stare first and looked away. "I threw them away, Mother. I flushed them, okay?"

Carol watched her a moment longer, then sighed with obvious exasperation as she turned to Carson and Serena. "I don't know how to thank you. I'm sorry you've been dragged into our dirty little family problems like this."

There was an edge to her voice that made Carson uncomfortable. "Everybody has problems, Carol," he assured her. "Sometimes we need friends to help us sort things out, give us a shoulder to lean on. I've got to tell you, I've been praying hard since Jenny's call tonight. And I'll continue to—"

"Can we go home now?" Kirby's whole demeanor had changed. Her voice sounded abrasive, and Carson thought he detected that same edge to her voice that he'd heard in Carol's.

"First, don't you think you should apologize to Carson and Serena for dragging them out here like this?" Carol asked.

"I didn't drag them, Mother, they came out by themselves."

Carol shot her daughter another sharp glance, and the mutual antagonism was palpable.

This time it was Carol who broke the staring contest. "Fine, let's go home. We'll talk about this later."

three

Serena awoke Friday morning just as dawn broke through the big bay window of her master bedroom. She slid from between rose-colored satin sheets and pulled the covers back to let the bed air. Later, when she was fully awake, she would make the bed so Blythe wouldn't feel compelled to do it for her.

She crept barefoot across the amethyst Berber carpet to a long, low chest of drawers, the color of ocean driftwood. After selecting a black, one-piece bathing suit from a drawer, she slid out of her silky nightgown and pulled on the suit. Emily would come running through the house in a few moments, waking everyone up, cheerful and laughing. But Serena wanted to talk with Jenny first. She had still been upset about Kirby last night.

"Jenny," she called softly, pausing to glance through the open door at her pretty seventeen year old. "Honey, are you awake?"

Jenny stirred. A few tresses of her long, dark brown hair tumbled across her face, and she sniffed as a curl tickled her nose. She opened almond-shaped, golden brown eyes and gazed up at Serena.

"Morning, Mom."

Serena smiled indulgently at her daughter. "Good morning." Jenny looked fine this morning, not worried or upset. Perhaps the talk could wait.

Jenny stretched her long, slender arms over her head and yawned loudly. "I suppose you're going to drag me out of bed and throw me in that icy pool."

As she spoke, Emily Ann, her thirteen-year-old sister, came

23

dashing down the hallway to stand beside Serena. Emily's grin was filled with mischief. "Yes, and I'm going to help." She was already dressed in her own modest suit, and her short, muscular legs carried her quickly to her sister's bed. She grasped the covers and flung them back. "Come on, sleepyhead, up!" Tossing her long hair behind her shoulders, she bounded on top of Jenny and tickled her.

"Okay, I'm up!" Jenny cried. "Emily!" she protested over her sister's giggles. "If you don't stop it, I'll dunk you when we get to the pool!"

Emily's soft brown eyes danced with glee. "You'll have to catch me first!" She dashed out of the room and down the hall. Seconds later there was a loud splash from the pool in back.

Serena and Jenny followed. As the three laughed and played in the water, the day warmed quickly.

A door closed on the private apartment attached to the house, and they turned to watch Blythe pass by in her gardening clothes, carrying a pair of trimming shears in her hand. Emily climbed from the pool and showered her grandmother with drops of water as she squeezed her long strands of brown hair. "Granny, aren't you swimming with us this morning?"

"Not this morning, Honey." Blythe set down the shears and tucked an old white tee shirt into the waistband of her jeans. "I want to get to work on that garden before the sun gets too hot." The skin around her eyes creased as she frowned and glanced around the yard. "Now, where did that pup get to? Rascal! Where are you?" She wandered off toward her huge garden, which overflowed with vegetables.

"Uh-oh." Emily Ann pointed toward the rose bushes at the side of the house.

Rascal poked his muddy nose out from beneath a bush as he rolled in the damp earth, his golden blond coat no longer gold, but muddy brown. Serena and her daughters watched as Blythe let out a howl of dismay and darted after the pup.

Rascal sped by the pool, missing the edge by a mere few inches, with Blythe no more than half a step behind him.

"Emily Ann Van Buren," she yelled as she passed by them. "If you find any more abandoned puppies in the ditch, just leave them there! Their owners know what they're doing!"

Emily giggled unrepentantly, then sighed when they all heard a yelp coming from the middle of the garden. "Poor Rascal."

Jenny snorted. "Don't worry about 'poor Rascal.' You should see Granny with him when no one else is around. I caught her feeding him a steak once. She even cut it up into bite-sized pieces so he could eat it better, and when she saw me watching, she turned red and jabbered something about the steak not smelling just right."

"Maybe it didn't."

"Granny had brought that steak home from the butcher the day before. If it didn't smell right, she'd have taken it back and demanded a fresh cut." Jenny chuckled as the pup emerged from the garden, his big, dark eyes darting from Serena, to Jenny, to Emily in a campaign for sympathy.

"Speaking of steak," Emily suggested, "why don't I fix steak and eggs for breakfast while you two get ready for work?"

As Emily climbed out of the pool to run, dripping wet, into the house, Jenny turned over on her back and floated out into the middle of the pool.

Serena watched her daughter thoughtfully as she began her water exercises. Jenny was so pretty—prettier than Serena had been at her age. Serena hoped she was also more mature. "Honey, are you still planning to go to the clinic this afternoon after you get off work?"

Water splashed as Jenny straightened. "What? The clinic? Oh, Mom, do I have to? A bunch of the kids are going down to the lake this afternoon, and I want to go."

"Of course you don't have to; that's why it's called 'volunteer work.' I just thought. . .well. . .I'd hoped. . ."

Jenny squinted at her in the sunlight, then her expression cleared. "Is Kirby going to the clinic today?" she asked softly.

Serena didn't reply. As a physician, she protected the confidentiality of her patients. As a mother, she wanted to share this information with her worried daughter, and Kirby was not her patient.

"Oh. You're doing the silent thing because of privacy rules. I got it. Of course I'll be there. I can leave for the lake afterward. Let's go get breakfast before Blythe feeds it to Rascal."

&

The traffic light turned yellow as Serena approached the intersection. She sped up to cross before it turned red. She glanced sideways at Jenny. "Who was going to go to the lake with you this afternoon?"

"I don't know for sure. Danny said some of his buddies are going with their girlfriends."

Serena felt that old familiar worry tugging at her common sense. "Danny?"

Jenny shot her mother a long-suffering look. "So what if he is going?"

Serena pulled up to the curb in front of the print shop where Jenny worked three days a week. "But there are other kids going, aren't there? You know how I feel about you spending too much time alone with Danny."

"Oh, Mom, of course there are other kids going. At least, I'm sure there must be; Danny said there were." She climbed out of the van and shook several tendrils of hair back from her face. "Besides, you and Danny's mom are old friends. Don't you trust us?" She closed the door without waiting for an answer.

Serena watched her walk into the shop. "Yes, Jenny, I trust you," she whispered. "But I'm not sure I trust Danny Scott, even if Paula is my oldest friend." Making a mental note to call Paula later, Serena pulled back out into the traffic and drove toward work.

❧

"Good morning, Dr. Van Buren," Serena's secretary-receptionist greeted.

"Hi, Gail. You're early this morning. Did you get your car fixed?"

"Finally!" Gail grinned up at her, then stood and followed Serena into the inner office. "The phone's already been ringing for you this morning. It promises to be a hectic day."

"Of course," Serena replied dryly. "It's Friday, and we all wanted off early tonight." She sat down at her desk and shuffled through some papers left from the night before. "Messages?"

Gail pulled a watering can from the cupboard by the sink and watered Serena's jungle of plant life around the office. "Dr. Tanner called first thing. He wants to discuss last night's incident." She looked up from her work. "What happened last night?"

The buzzer sounded at the front desk, and Serena waved Gail from the room. "I'll tell you about it when we get a break this morning."

"You mean if we get a break." Gail rushed out to answer the phone, closing the door behind her with a quiet swish.

Serena stared absently through the profuse growth of plants around the window to the large patch of blue sky outside. Would Kirby go to the clinic today, or would she allow her mother to convince her to have another abortion? If only Serena could talk to Carol for Kirby, if she could make her understand the pain Kirby was going through.

The private line buzzed, and Serena pressed the button to talk into the tiny, oblong speaker. "Yes, this is Dr. Van Buren, may I help you?" She picked up her pen and made a notation on one of the charts in front of her.

"Yes, you may, but what concerns me is whether you will." It was Carson's deep voice.

Serena felt a spontaneous smile warm her face. "That all depends on what you need."

"Well, it's a long story. I guess I need a sounding board."

There was an edge of worry in his voice, and Serena grew serious. "Is it about Kirby? Have you heard from her this morning?"

"Would you meet me for lunch? I hate to talk about this over the telephone."

Serena glanced at her schedule. "Sorry, but I can't today. I'll just have time for a quick sandwich at noon—if that."

"Probably not even that. Serena, you work yourself too hard."

Serena knew her family would agree. "I've cut my hours here at the office so I can spend more time at Alternative, but it seems as if my patient load hasn't eased."

"Have dinner with me tonight. We can talk about Kirby then. You can't possibly have patients around the clock."

"Okay, okay, I give up! What time, and where should I meet you?"

"Seven o'clock at your house. Good-bye, Serena."

The line disconnected, and Serena shook her head in exasperation, unable to control a playful smile that teased her lips.

She liked Carson. She had even had more than a twinge or two of physical attraction for him—after all, he was an attractive and strong man. Better yet, a compassionate man. In ways, he reminded her of Jennings; in other ways, the two were nothing alike. She couldn't deny the surge of excitement she felt at the opportunity to spend time with a man whom she had begun to admire deeply in the past few months, but there was an emotional barrier she had promised herself never to cross again.

The phone buzzed again, scattering her thoughts. This time it was Paula Scott, Danny's mother, Serena's oldest friend.

"Paula, I was just going to call you," Serena greeted her friend warmly.

"Oh, yeah?" Paula's casual voice came through the speaker. "I bet I can guess why. Is Jenny going to the lake with that monster of mine tonight?"

"Of course. Do you think she'd pass up a chance like that?"

"No, but do you know if any of the other kids are going?"

"Jenny said they were." Serena's earlier sense of foreboding returned. "Why? Do you have reason to believe they aren't?"

"If my son finds a chance to get Jenny alone, he'll take it. He's just like his father was at his age," she muttered.

Feeling old and tired all of a sudden, Serena leaned back in her chair and sighed. "I don't know, Paula. What are we supposed to do with them? Unfortunately, they're just like we were."

"Yeah, and look at the trouble it landed us." Paula echoed Serena's sigh. "The thing is, I can't keep Danny from going. He's eighteen, going on twenty-five, and he has his own car. If I try to stop him, we'll just get into a fight that won't solve a thing, and he would say, 'What's the matter, Mom, don't you trust me?'"

In spite of herself, Serena chuckled. "Where have I heard that before?"

"I think we invented the phrase." Paula paused thoughtfully. "Let me call some of Danny's friends' mothers and see if the other kids really are going. If they aren't, I can alert you."

"Then I can have another talk with Jenny. Paula, do you think we're overreacting because of our own mistakes?"

"Maybe just a little, but look at it this way," Paula argued, "if your mother had talked with you about things the way you talk with Jenny, maybe you wouldn't have that past. If mine had, maybe I wouldn't, either." Paula had married Danny's father just two months before Danny was born.

"I have to hang up now. My first patient just arrived."

As always when with her patients, Serena became totally involved with her work, and the day sped by. She loved her job, loved working with people. She earned a good income, and she channeled much of it into the Alternative Clinic downtown. Jennings had left the family well provided for and had taken out a generous insurance policy several years before his death. The interest from that investment helped keep Alternative going.

Situated as it was on High Street, with a teeming population surrounding it, Alternative attracted many young—and even older—pregnant women. Initially, curiosity brought them in. Word had spread in the past few years. More people were learning the value of new life.

❧

Serena stepped into the comfortably air-conditioned interior of Alternative late that afternoon and saw her older daughter in the waiting room, sorting through a box of newly donated baby clothes.

"Hi, Honey. Has anyone come in yet?"

Jenny shrugged. "No, but Kirby should soon. I called her and told her I'd be here. We had a long talk, and she told me her parents are still really upset about last night." She frowned at her mother. "Aren't you off early?"

"I had a patient cancel the final appointment of the day. Are you still planning to go to the lake?"

Jenny bowed her head and sighed. "No. They wanted to spend the night, and I didn't think you'd let me since there were guys going, too."

"Good thinking, Sweetheart." Serena walked over and sat down to help with the sorting. "Was Danny angry when you told him you weren't going?"

Jenny nodded in silence, and sadness was evident on her face.

"I'm sorry." Serena reached over and lay a hand over Jenny's hands. "I know it's hard, and I'm glad you had the strength to say no. So many girls don't."

Jenny grimaced. "That's why you have this place, but that doesn't make it much easier to turn Danny down. I really like him, and. . .and. . ."

"Growing up isn't easy."

Jenny shook her head. "Making the right decisions isn't easy."

They finished folding the clothes in companionable silence, and Serena stacked them in the back storage room. They often received donated clothing, baby items, and even personal care products for the women who were in need. As word had spread over the years about Alternative, more and more people supported them.

About twenty minutes later, the chimes played as the front door of the clinic opened, and Serena and Jenny both turned to find Kirby hesitantly stepping inside. They both got up to greet her, and her relief was evident.

Jenny walked over and gave her friend a long, hard hug. "I was beginning to think you'd chickened out."

Kirby's blue-eyed gaze darted around the clinic. "I almost did."

"Well, you're here now," Serena said. "I'll call Sharon from the back. She's our nurse on duty today."

Kirby tensed. "Can Jenny come with me?"

"Sure, she can."

"Mother doesn't know anything about this, but she wouldn't shut up about it last night or this morning. I'm just glad she had to go to work today. If I'm not home before she gets off work, I'm dead. I can't wait around for the results. Can I call you?"

"Why don't you think about coming back in Monday?" Serena asked.

Kirby groaned. "That long? Do I have to come in?"

"I'd like for you to," Serena said. "Are you forgetting that we're in this thing together? I want to be here with you to help you through it. There will be plans to make, and if the test is positive, we'll want to make arrangements for a medical examination."

"But can't you do that?" Kirby asked. "You're an OB/Gyn."

"But I'm your friend, first. In order to avoid a conflict of interest, I'll arrange for another physician to do the exam."

Kirby's gaze flicked to Jenny nervously.

"It's okay, Kirby," Jenny said. "Come on. Let's go find Sharon."

&a

Later, after Kirby left and the clinic was locked, Jenny stepped up beside Serena and watched through the window as traffic passed by on the street outside. "Mom, what would you do if I were pregnant?"

Serena thought about that for a moment, as she had many times before. "All I can say for sure is what I wouldn't do. I wouldn't panic and scream and hurl accusations at you. I would want to be there for you. And you know how I feel about abortion. Of course, the real question is, what would you do?"

A bemused smile crossed Jenny's face. "I'd tell you. Some girls can't say that about their mothers. Most of my friends' mothers would have panicked if they'd even asked the question."

"Most of the girls' mothers don't work with pregnant teenagers every day."

Jenny cocked her head to the side and frowned. "Some of them are volunteers here, remember? Jannell's daughter's in my class in school. There's just something different about you. You understand. Do you think it's different for us because you adopted Emily and me?"

Serena blinked at her in surprise. "No, Honey, I don't think so. What on earth made you think about that?"

Jenny shrugged and went to get her purse. "I don't know, I guess lately I've been trying to see the differences between adopted children and natural children. I know Danny's getting tired of hearing it." She shrugged, as if the subject didn't occupy too many of her thoughts. "Are we going home now? I'm hungry."

They drove through the heavy, noisy Jefferson City traffic in silence. It wasn't until they neared the suburbs that Jenny turned to look at Serena. "Mom, you know, I was just thinking. . .if you kept the clinic open later, you could reach more people."

"I considered that, but I'd have to pay someone a hefty salary to stay downtown at night. Let's face it: I may make good money and your father may have left us a safety net; but there isn't enough to double salaries, and I'm trying to cut my hours at work."

"Ask for donations," Jenny suggested. A mischievous expression crossed her face. "Or marry Carson Tanner."

Serena rolled her eyes. "Jenny Van Buren, wherever did you get an idea like that?"

Jenny eyed Serena innocently. "Well, Mom, don't you two see each other a lot?"

"I haven't gone out with him in at least a couple of months." She neglected to mention she was seeing him tonight. That was about Kirby.

"I don't know why not. He's gorgeous—that is, for an older man."

Serena parked in the driveway and climbed out. "You sound like your granny."

Jenny's golden brown eyes shone as she stepped ahead of her mother and threw open the front door. "How many times have you known Granny to be wrong?" she asked with a teasing grin. "Hi, everybody! We're home! Is dinner ready? I'm starved!"

four

Serena felt like a girl on her first date when she opened the front door to find Carson standing there. Evidently, he hadn't worked today, because he looked well rested and relaxed— not like a man who'd been rushing from patient to patient in a busy emergency room all day. He was dressed casually in jeans and a royal blue pullover that seemed to reflect the deep blue-black of his hair. The gauzy material of her dress floated around her legs as she turned to lead him inside.

It was a very obvious coincidence when, just at that moment, Blythe came through the back door, followed by Rascal. Blythe's bespectacled gaze zoomed in on Carson, and she gave him a delighted smile. "Hello, Carson Tanner! Haven't seen you around here for a while." She took a swipe at her perspiring face and cast a warning glance at Rascal, who had a habit of sniffing legs.

"It's good to see you again, Mrs. Van Buren," Carson replied, his dark eyes warm and sincere. "It has been a while, but you know Serena. Right now, she's calling the shots."

Blythe walked toward them, then stopped and leaned forward conspiratorially. "Don't worry, I haven't given up hope for you." She shot Serena a challenging stare.

Serena glared back. Time to get out of here before Blythe could embarrass her further. "I'll get my purse and be ready to go. It'll just take me a second, Carson." As she dashed down the carpeted hallway, she heard Emily's voice.

"Hi, Carson! Welcome back. Are you and Mom going out on a date?"

Serena stepped into her bedroom before she heard the

reply, but she couldn't miss the sound of Emily's footsteps pattering down the hallway to her sister's room.

"Jenny, he's here! He's here!" she squealed, with childish unconcern about the fact that her voice was loud enough to reverberate all the way through the house. She slammed into Jenny's bedroom, and Serena heard their muted giggles.

With a sigh of exasperation, Serena closed her own bedroom door and leaned against it. In any other situation, she could deal with Carson on a strictly professional level, but it was impossible to behave professionally when her well-meaning family persisted in pushing her into a romantic situation with a man who, she had told them time after time, was merely a friend and colleague. What made it difficult was the fact that he had known all of them before he knew Serena. He was their friend, too, and he often saw them at church, was closely involved in their lives as the girls' youth leader.

So why had she allowed him to pick her up here? He had given her no chance to refuse, but couldn't she have called him back? She sighed. She was always telling her girls not to say "if only," but "next time." Next time she would know better.

She stepped over to the mirror and fluffed the silvery curls of her hair. The problem was, her family—and perhaps Carson—were far too astute. He unsettled her. Jennings had been gone too long, and there were many things about Carson that fascinated her. She needed better control.

❧

Carson felt like one of Dr. Doolittle's Pushme-Pullyou animals. Half the time he could feel the attraction emanating from Serena; the other half she very politely told him to back off. He knew she was confused right now. She undoubtedly still felt married to Jennings in some ways, even though he'd been gone three years. The grief would never disappear completely, but the living had to keep living. How did he tell Serena all of this?

He'd been intrigued by her from the first time he met her. She was so warm and vibrant, so caring about others. The more he knew about her, the more he learned to care for her, and he already loved her family.

Blythe had told him a lot about Serena's past, things that Serena would never have divulged. Blythe was the one who told Carson about Serena's intensity over her work and about the nights she sat up in the family room, staring out into the darkness, unable to sleep for worrying about her patients. Through Blythe, Carson had learned that Serena often came home in tears after leaving the clinic, heartbroken because she had failed with one of her patients at Alternative.

"You two have fun, now," Blythe said as she followed Serena and Carson out to the front porch. "It's Friday night; no need to be in early."

Serena replied dryly, "Thanks, I'll remember that."

Carson chuckled as he preceded Serena toward his midnight blue Saturn in her driveway.

"Is something funny, Dr. Tanner?"

The chuckle turned into a full-throated laugh as Carson fell into step beside her and laid a casual arm across her shoulders. "Serena, you have a great family. For a mature woman, you certainly let them get the better of you. You and I are not opponents. Why don't you relax?" He helped her into the car and held her gaze. "You have nothing to fear from me."

"Of course you can see I'm terrified," she said.

Carson didn't stop in Jefferson City, but drove west on Highway 54. The beauty of the countryside increased with each mile, flaunting its rolling, tree-covered hills and squared patches of green and gold, jeweled with farm ponds and dotted with huge round bales of hay. The serenity of the changing scenes seemed to ease something within Serena. When Carson glanced across at her, she had leaned back in her seat, a soft smile curving her lips.

She caught him looking at her. "Where are we going tonight?"

"I know a place, hidden in the trees, a few minutes' drive from here. It has excellent food and a peaceful atmosphere. You look like you could use some relaxation."

"Always the flatterer, aren't you? This place isn't, by chance, on a shore of the Lake of the Ozarks, is it?"

"My secret is out."

"Then I hate to tell you this, but it's more than just a few minutes' drive."

"It won't seem that long. A quiet drive is what we both need after last night."

"I thought you needed to talk about Kirby."

"Later, if you don't mind. It's a situation that worries me, and I don't want to lose my appetite."

As he drove, Carson darted a quick glance at Serena's profile. She could pass for a woman of twenty-two more easily than a woman of thirty-seven with two teenaged daughters. Perhaps that was because she was always so active. She didn't give herself time to brood.

"How's the clinic?" he asked, knowing that was one of the closest things to her heart besides her family. But that wasn't the only reason he was interested in Alternative. The idea of a clinic that produced a loving alternative to abortion, offering adoption services for childless couples, had appealed to him from the beginning. In fact, he'd donated anonymously through the church several times in the past.

"Busy. We've had a lot of girls come in lately. One of them was fourteen years old. You should have seen the look of relief on her face when she discovered the test results were negative." She shook her head. "Unfortunately, she could be pregnant in a month or so. It's almost as if the girls think they're immune to pregnancy. It's so difficult to convince a young girl about the dangers out there." Serena shook her head again. "How do you convince a know-it-all teenager that even if she never gets pregnant, the emotional scars she gets from her promiscuity will be with her for the rest of her life?"

"Not to mention diseases that could kill her." He paused. "I'm worried about Kirby."

"I thought you weren't going to talk about her until after dinner."

"Sorry, I can't help it. I called their house tonight and caught them while they were having dinner. I didn't talk long, but I could hear the tension in their voices. Carol seems like a woman on the edge—but then, she's been that way ever since I met them two years ago. I hate to think Kirby is picking up on her mother's habits, but sometimes she sounds just like her."

"I don't know Carol or Hal that well," Serena said. "Kirby's been to the house a few times, a few sleepovers with Jenny, and she's good company."

"Do you ever wonder about the influence she might have on Jenny?"

"Of course, but Jenny isn't easily swayed."

He drove in silence a few more moments, then said, "I want to be with Kirby when she tells her parents she's pregnant."

"I think you should be."

"I just hope I say and do the right thing."

"Don't worry. You have a way with people." She turned and grinned up at him. "Especially women."

Carson had to concentrate on the road, but he felt broadsided by her mischievous smile and penetrating gaze. "You're a woman, and I don't seem to be making any headway with you."

"What do you call this date? You talked me into it, didn't you? And I don't date."

"Okay, I'm sorry. I take it back. I have you under my spell." He grew serious. "Alternative is a godsend, and you're the perfect person to have it."

"Sometimes I feel as if I'm just treading water."

"You do more than you know. You're good with Kirby and great with Jenny and Emily Ann. Your work with Alternative is enjoyable, isn't it? You're not having any problems?"

Serena leaned her head back against the headrest and stared out of the window. "No problems with the clinic."

"Could you use another helper? A counselor? Or floor sweeper?"

She glanced at him with renewed interest. "I could always use help at the clinic."

"Is a man allowed?"

"Allowed? That would be wonderful! Jenny was just telling me tonight that I should keep the clinic open later, but I don't think we can afford more salaries."

Carson's mind shot ahead. He could do something to help her there, too, but he wouldn't say anything about it just now. "Tell me," he said instead, "have you thought about Kirby staying with you if she needs to?"

Serena blinked at him in surprise. "Yes, of course she can stay with me. Why? Do you think Carol will throw her out?"

"I don't know, but it's a possibility if Kirby decides to go through with the pregnancy. She will need a lot of love and understanding."

Serena hesitated for a moment before answering. "I can give her that," she said quietly.

He turned off the main highway onto a narrow country road. "I don't doubt that for a moment, Serena."

The late evening sun had disappeared behind a thick growth of lush forest. Carson pressed a button, and the tinted windows of the car silently slid down. Serena took a deep breath. "Mm-m-m, smell that. No exhaust fumes, no smoke stacks, just fresh, country air."

They came to a break in the trees, and Carson stopped the car for a moment. A green valley stretched out in front of them. Vivid blues and soft pinks coursed in and around the clouds. Serena sat as if transfixed by the beauty.

"God's artwork," Carson murmured. "Not only do we see it, but we experience it with all our senses. It makes me want to hold a worship service right here."

Some of the enchantment disappeared from Serena's expression. "It is beautiful, all right."

Carson took his foot from the brake and allowed the car to coast down the steep hill again.

Serena turned sideways in her seat and regarded Carson thoughtfully. "How long have you been working with the church youth?"

"I started teaching Sunday school when we lived in Columbia thirteen years ago, when I was twenty-eight. Does that tell you how old I am?"

"Forty-one."

The tree line ended abruptly, and he slowed the car as they looked across the wide expanse of the Lake of the Ozarks. Serena gasped appreciatively as she stared across the glittering water, where millions of pink diamonds reflected the rosy hues of the lingering sunset.

"I'd forgotten how beautiful it is," she murmured.

"Has it been that long since you were here?" Carson followed the road that curved around the shoreline.

"The last time was just before Jennings died. The girls and I haven't been back since."

"My wife and I used to come here, too," Carson said. They rode in silence for a moment. He gazed out at the water as poignant memories forced their way through his mind—the calls and laughter of the boaters; the boats, themselves, the sounds of their motors echoing across the valley; the mossy, slightly fishy scents of the water; and the ever-present green of the trees that surrounded it.

Serena looked up as a pontoon passed by them in the water.

"We used to have a boat a lot like that one." She smiled. "The motor was so powerful, two people could ski behind it. If we'd known how much danger Jennings was in when he exerted himself like that, we'd never have bought the boat in the first place."

Carson knew Jennings had died of a heart attack. "He was so young, Serena. No one could have predicted it."

"One moment he was out mowing the lawn, seemingly healthy and vigorous, and the next moment he was lying on the ground without the strength to call for help. It was a shock."

"Jenny and Emily have come a long way since then," Carson said. He wanted to ask Serena why she hadn't, but he decided to keep his mouth shut for once.

They pulled up to an A-frame building with redwood siding, and Carson parked. "Hungry?"

"Starved."

"Then let's go in."

❧

The Secret Cove specialized in seafood and steaks, and Serena quickly discovered that it was everything Carson had promised it would be, in service, as well as in the deliciously cooked food. She ordered fresh rainbow trout and was not disappointed.

They spent the first few minutes eating silently, savoring each bite of the expertly cooked dishes. Quiet music played in the background, and the tables in the dining area were set far enough apart to give the illusion of privacy. Tall red candles, crowned by dancing flames, supplied the lighting. More than once, Serena glanced across the glow of the candles to find Carson studying her, and she glanced quickly away again, unwilling to be drawn by the magnetism she felt emanating from him.

"Has Blythe lived with you long?" Carson asked, finally breaking the silence.

"Since Jennings died. The girls and I invited her to live with us right after the funeral. She refused." Serena smiled at the memory. "She said she'd lived alone too long. She didn't want to be a burden to anyone. It was Jenny's idea to build an apartment onto the house, and it worked." She spread her hands in the air. "Blythe's been with us ever since, and I haven't heard a hint of regret from anyone. Of course, she didn't take my husband's place, but having her there helped fill a void for all of us. Blythe is a wonderful friend."

Carson pushed back slightly from the table after he finished his bass. "Yes, she is. You were especially blessed. But then, so was she, to have you," he added quietly. "The death of a loved one is final and debilitating. I know—I lost my wife five years ago in an automobile accident."

Serena put down her fork and folded her napkin. "I'm sorry. I heard you had lost your wife, but I never felt comfortable asking about it."

He inclined his head as dessert arrived. As they slowly savored the rich, creamy chocolate cheesecake, Carson entertained Serena with humorous cases he'd had in the ER—without divulging names, of course. He kept her laughing until they were halfway home.

By this time, the sky was aglow with stars and a thin sliver of new moon. Carson left the windows of the car open, and Serena loved the silky soft feel of the night air against her bare arms. The sounds of tiny night creatures from the forest reached her ears, and the warm scent of a full-blown summer drifted and flowed with the breeze.

"Serena," Carson said at last, his tone growing serious, "I've been wondering something for a long time, and if you think it's none of my business, tell me."

"What's that?"

"The reason I think it might be my business is because of Jenny and Emily. I've grown to care very much for them these last couple of years—I care for all the kids in my youth group, but there's something special about—"

"You want to know why I don't go to church," Serena said.

He glanced at her quickly. "I don't want to offend you."

"You aren't. I'm not sure I can answer your question, though, because I'm not sure of the answer, myself."

"Is it too painful?"

Serena met his gaze honestly. "You could be right, there is some pain involved in going."

"Three years' worth?" he asked gently.

Serena sat without answering for a few moments. There were old wounds there, much older than three years. It had been a very long time since she had actually enjoyed attending church services. Such a very long time. . .

She looked straight ahead at the road. "More than that," she said softly. "Maybe when I figure it out myself, I'll try to explain it to you."

When he slowed the car and turned onto her street, she felt his gaze rest on her for a long moment, and she felt like she was in high school again, coming home from her first date. Would he try to kiss her? Would he ask her out again? Everything within her dreamed that he would, yet the protective shield in her mind hoped he wouldn't. When they pulled into the driveway, she sat where she was, as if she'd been bolted to the seat.

"You have a wonderfully warm, embracing nature, Serena Van Buren," he declared softly, the deep, vibrating sound of his voice striking a chord of excitement in her heart. He took her hand in a gentle grip, but she still refused to meet his gaze. "When do you plan to start living your life again?"

Serena closed her eyes briefly. "I'm living my life."

"Through others, maybe, but not for yourself. Every patient you see receives a healthy dose of your compassion and understanding, but you have needs, too." He raised his other hand and traced the outline of her face with his fingers.

She shivered and pulled away. "Don't you do the same thing? It's been five years for you, and you haven't remarried." Her voice sounded shaky and unsure to her own ears.

His hand fell away, and the white gleam of his teeth revealed his sense of humor. "At least I'm making an effort to join the ranks of the living again. You're not helping me," he complained.

The warm strength of his voice seemed to spread an overpowering current of electricity through her whole body, and for a few seconds, against her will, she felt the urge to yield to his magnetism. With a burst of willpower, she pulled away and stepped out of the car. Taking a deep breath, she closed her eyes for a moment to steady herself.

"Goodnight, Carson," she said firmly as he climbed from his seat and came across to walk her to the door. "Thank you for—"

"Thank you, Serena," he said softly as he grasped her hand once more and raised it to his mouth.

She felt the shock of the tingling warmth of his lips to the tips of her fingers, then he released her and walked with her to the front porch. After she let herself inside, closed the door behind her, and stepped into the dark foyer, she heard a muffled giggle.

"Hi, Mom!" came a cheerful voice from out of the darkness.

Serena smiled. "Emily Ann, is that you?" Something slimy and wet touched her ankle, and she recognized the rough warmth of Rascal's tongue. She stepped down into the sunken living room and felt her way across to the sofa. "Why are you sitting in here in the dark?" She reached over and switched on a lamp. When she turned back toward the sofa, she discovered that Jenny was curled on the sofa in her nightgown, too. Both girls grinned broadly.

"We didn't want Carson to think we were waiting up for

you," Jenny said sleepily. "How come you're home so early?"

Serena sat down on the cushion beside Jenny and slid her high-heeled sandals from her feet, fighting Rascal at every move. "It isn't early. What do you consider late?"

"Come on, Mom. I usually get home later than this when I go out," Jenny complained. "It's only eleven o'clock. What's the matter—don't you like him?"

"Of course I like him, Sweetheart. He's an excellent person and a great youth leader."

"Mom, that's not what Jenny means, and you know it!" Emily exclaimed.

Serena aimed a playful tap at her daughter's shoulder and stood up.

"No, wait, Mom," Jenny pleaded. "We've been talking about it tonight. . . ." She patted the sofa in an invitation for Serena to sit back down.

With a wry grin, Serena looked at each daughter in turn. "What have you been talking about?" She sank down between the two.

Both were silent for a moment, and Serena waited patiently, already aware of what they were trying to say. She was touched by it, but also a little disturbed. Once again, they were getting their hopes up about Carson. They obviously adored him and talked about him all the time.

Jenny finally spoke, her young face serious. "I guess maybe we're different from a lot of families, aren't we? I mean we're pretty close."

Serena nodded. "Yes, Honey, we're very close. We share a lot of love between us. I've been blessed a thousand times over with you two."

"But it's you, Mom," Jenny insisted. "You're the blessing in this family. If you and Daddy hadn't told us from the time we were little, we would never have guessed we were adopted. You've shown us the kind of love a lot of kids don't get from their own flesh-and-blood parents. You're the best thing that could ever have happened to us."

Serena grinned at her older daughter. "You can say that after you missed going to the lake because of me today?"

Jenny looked away. "It wasn't because of you, Mom." She glanced quickly at Emily. "There were other things involved. Besides, we've never been back to the lake since Daddy died, and I thought maybe I would wait until we could go as a family again."

"What Jenny's trying to tell you, Mom," Emily stated impatiently, "is that we don't mind if you marry Carson and make us a family again."

"Emily!" Jenny cried. "You have no tact! You weren't supposed to put it like that!" She turned to Serena. "What we are trying to say is that we want you to be happy. Daddy's been gone a while now, and I know kids don't take the place of a husband, no matter how much they love you. You don't have to worry about us getting upset if you ever do decide to get married again. We just wanted you to know that."

"Yeah, we just wanted you to know that," Emily echoed her sister's words, looking up at her mother uncertainly.

"I do know that," Serena assured them. "But you need to understand that we are a family just the way we are now. I don't have to have a man in my life to fulfill me. We take care of each other, right?"

Jenny frowned. "Yes, but there's something to be said for men, too, isn't there? I mean, don't we need a chance to learn how to live with males as well as females?"

"There's not much difference." She squeezed them both tightly, then sat back, with an arm around each girl. "Speaking of families, I have something to ask you, and I want you to think hard about this, because it affects us as a family."

Both girls sat up eagerly.

"No, it's not about my getting married again. It's about a

teenager who's in trouble and may need a place to stay for a while."

"You mean stay here?" Emily asked.

Jenny tucked her feet beneath her nightgown and huddled closer to Serena. "Is it Kirby? Have you talked to her? I told Emily about it. If that pregnancy test is positive, her parents will freak."

"I hope not. Maybe Carson can work things out with her parents. I'll talk to your granny tomorrow."

"You know it'll be okay with her," Emily said.

"I'm sure it will be, but this is her home, too, and she should have a chance to give her permission."

Jenny kissed her mother and went to bed, but Emily lingered in the living room. "Mom, did you say you and Carson are both working on Kirby's parents?"

"Well, I'm not sure 'working on' is the phrase I'd use, but yes, we're both very concerned with the welfare of this family."

"You and Carson do work well together, don't you?"

"I suppose we do, why?"

"Oh, I was just wondering. Don't worry—with you both working with Kirby's parents, they're bound to come around. Good night, Mom."

"Good night, Emily."

five

Carson dragged himself out of bed Saturday morning to answer the strident ring of the phone. He'd intended to get up early, but not quite this early. It was barely light outside. He answered sleepily.

"Carson, you've got to help me. Talk to them! I can't take this!" It was Kirby Acuff's voice, choked with sobs, and it brought Carson totally awake.

"Kirby, what's wrong? Where are you?"

"I'm at home, but I won't be here long if this keeps up. I'll do it again, and no one'll stop me this time."

Carson could hear yelling in the background. It sounded like Carol. "What's going on there? Tell me what's happening."

"It's Mother. She forced me to tell her that I might be pregnant again."

"How did she force you?"

"She wore me down. She's been up all night long crying, pacing the floor, yelling at me. She's. . .she's crazy! I need you to talk to her!"

"All night?"

"Yes!"

Carson sighed and glanced down at a number beside his telephone. If Kirby was in an abusive situation, he could call the police to go to the house and remove her; but unless there was physical abuse, few people would take him seriously. "Kirby, listen to me. Calm down. Are you—"

"Please talk to Mom. I can't handle her by myself."

He could hear Carol Acuff's voice getting louder, heard muffled sobs, then Carol's angry voice came over the line.

"Carson Tanner, is that you?" she snapped. "Nobody bothered to tell me my own daughter's pregnant again! How could you deceive us like this?"

"I did nothing to deceive you. I planned to be there when Kirby told you. Do you understand what your reaction is doing to Kirby right now, Carol?"

"That's none of your business! I'm just talking some sense into her that she should have had in the first place!"

"I'm coming to your house now."

There was a long silence, and then the sound of agonized crying. "How could this happen again? We did everything we could to keep her from. . .oh, how could she do this to us?"

"Calm down," Carson said gently. "You need to take some deep breaths and give yourself time to think." He spoke with her as he would speak to one of the teenagers in his church youth group. "Why don't you sit down for a few quiet moments? I'll get dressed and come over so we can talk about th—"

"No." Her voice was firm. "Not here. Not now. I don't want anyone to see us like this."

Carson waited, holding the line, unwilling to release that tenuous connection to this desperate family that needed God's touch so badly. He heard Kirby's sobs in the distance, and Carol's quiet sniffles, and wondered where Hal was.

Hal Acuff was a quiet man with a quick sense of humor who allowed his wife to control their household. Carson wasn't one of those men who thought a man should be king at home—he loved the idea the Apostle Paul had in the Bible of mutual submission. Unfortunately, Carol never submitted, and part of the fault lay with Hal.

Eventually the sniffling subsided. Carson said softly, "Carol, are you sure you don't want me to come over? Sometimes it helps—"

"No." Her voice had regained some of its iron. "We know

what we have to do."

"Why don't we just wait until we can meet—"

"We'll go to the same place we went before."

"Is that Kirby's decision, Carol?"

"It's mine."

Carson curbed his growing anger. "It's Kirby's baby. Legally, she has total control over that life. Why don't you and Hal take Kirby down to the Alternative clinic Monday evening after you get off work. I'll come with you, and we can talk about it there."

"There's nothing to talk about. I've already made my decision."

"But Kirby hasn't made hers. She's the one who counts here." Carson forced his voice to remain calm. "The other night was a warning from Kirby. She was telling us that if she had to have another abortion, she wanted to die along with her baby. That's what she could—"

"Look, Carson, butt out, okay? I know how you and your church feel about abortion, and that's fine for you, but you don't have a teenager in your home who's about to ruin her life. Wait until you're in my situation before you start making any judgments."

Carson sighed wearily. "Fine. At least come with your daughter to the clinic Monday evening, if for no other reason than to make sure we don't 'poison' your daughter's mind further." He kept the sarcasm from his voice with difficulty.

There was a lengthy pause, then, "I'll be there."

"I'll tell Serena Van Buren to have a counselor waiting for us."

❧

The Saturday afternoon heat blasted down in waves from a cloudless sky. The luscious, fully ripe garden shimmered with layers of heated air, and the tiny, sparkling drops raining down from Blythe's hose scattered the sunlight into drifting rainbows. Serena settled back in her lounger and spread her arms over her head to catch more of the cooling drops. She watched with amusement as Rascal, sitting beside her, eyed one particular mud hole with careful nonchalance.

Slowly, cautiously, he rose to his feet and edged toward the tempting hole, all the time keeping an eye on Blythe's location in the garden. He opened his mouth and panted with anticipation as he lifted a paw to place it triumphantly in the water. . .but something went wrong.

With a loud shout, Blythe jumped from behind the tomato plants, wielding her trusty hose. With deadly accuracy, she caught Rascal in the face with a powerful stream of water, and he let out an indignant yelp before tucking his tail between his legs and streaking around the side of the house.

"Mongrel!" Blythe shouted after him as she walked over to the faucet to turn off the hose.

She pulled a bandana from her hip pocket and wiped it across her mud-streaked face, then pulled a pair of shiny metal pliers from another pocket and sat down beside Serena with the nozzle of the hose between her knees. "This thing's shooting sideways again," she muttered. Beneath her deft touch, and with the help of the pliers, the offending nozzle came apart.

"Rascal doesn't seem to think so," Serena replied dryly. "Blythe, you work too hard. Why don't you slow down?"

"What, and let this garden go to waste?" Blythe exclaimed. "That would be a shame, with all those kids starving in other countries." She shook her head. "Besides, what would I do if I didn't do this? I'm not one of those little old ladies who sit idly around drinking tea and eating cookies, waiting to die."

"You're not a little old lady, and I wasn't implying that."

Blythe worked a few seconds in silence, then glanced sideways at Serena. "The day I lose my usefulness is the day I hope the Lord takes me home."

"You'll never lose your usefulness around here."

"You're right, I won't. How will you and the girls manage after I'm gone?"

"You're not going anywhere. We need you too much." She paused thoughtfully. "Blythe, how would you feel if we invited another teenager to come and stay with us for awhile?"

Blythe blinked at her. "You're talking about Kirby? Jenny told me about her. I think that would be just fine."

"And knowing you, you'll try to pick her brain about all her family problems."

"I resent that! I'll just let her talk, and she'll know I care enough to listen. I'm no gossip."

Serena laid a conciliatory hand on Blythe's weathered arm. "I didn't say anything about gossiping. You care about people. That's one of the reasons I know we could help Kirby. Still, if she wants you to know about her problems, she'll have to tell you herself."

"Fine, then I'll pick your brain. How was the date last night?" Blythe shot Serena a sly glance and grinned.

Serena sighed. "The food was delicious; the drive down to the lake was peaceful, even if it did bring back a few memories."

"The lake?" Blythe stopped tinkering with the hose and peered at Serena over the rim of her glasses. "He took you to the lake? You don't call a drive like that romantic?"

Serena avoided Blythe's all too astute gaze. "Not in the least."

Blythe snorted. "Maybe not to you—"

"Hey, Mom!" Emily came out of the house in her swimsuit and ran barefoot across the wet grass. "My old speech teacher called. Remember Mrs. Jackson? She says there's going to be a school board meeting next Friday night, and she wants to know if you can attend and speak about Alternative for a few minutes. There's going to be a discussion group dealing with the problem of teenage pregnancy."

Serena reached up and smoothed long tendrils of hair away from her daughter's cheeks. She did remember Mrs. Jackson. She had been a volunteer at the clinic for a while, but her schedule was so busy, she'd had to bow out after about six weeks. Serena liked Bev Jackson.

"I suppose I could, but Mrs. Jackson could do a better job, and she knows a lot about Alternative."

"Please, Mom? She asked specifically for you." Emily lightly touched her mother's arm. "I already almost told her you'd do it. Besides, it's just for one night, and you've done it before." She glanced across at Blythe, and Serena could have sworn she detected a hidden signal pass between the two.

After a suspicious scrutiny of Blythe, Serena looked back down into her daughter's hopeful brown eyes and relented. "Okay, I'll do it. What time does it start?"

Emily launched into details, and Serena watched her youngest daughter's animated expressions with swelling love. This was her sunshine girl, brown-skinned and always laughing. Emily Ann was the one with the tender heart who had rescued Rascal from a muddy ditch. She'd then willingly turned him over to her grandmother—not because she was too lazy to care for him herself, but because she knew, instinctively, that the pup would brighten the older woman's life when the girls were off to school and Serena was at work.

Serena watched her daughter step across to the pool and dive in. Emily was also the mischievous one, and right now that child had something on her mind—some hidden project—and Serena could only wait helplessly to discover what it was.

She glanced sideways at her mother-in-law. "Is there really a meeting next Friday?"

Blythe's eyes widened. "Serena Van Buren! Are you accusing your own daughter of lying? I'd be ashamed."

Before long, both women joined Emily in the pool. For the next two hours, the summer heat had little effect on them. Before they were finished, the pool was completely sheltered by the shadows of the house, and the heat had begun to surrender to the evening—only slightly, but enough to make them feel pleasantly cool when a breeze touched their damp skin.

"May I fix dinner tonight, Mom?" Emily asked as she climbed from the pool. She shook her streaming hair back from her face and squeezed out the excess water. "I thought up a recipe for barbeque cups that should be fun."

"Be my guest," Serena invited gratefully. "I don't know where you get all that energy." She watched Emily pat herself sketchily with a beach towel, then run inside, still dripping.

With a sigh of fatigue, Blythe heaved herself onto the side of the pool. Serena followed.

"How many teenagers offer to help out in the kitchen?" Blythe asked, a glint of affection lighting up her blue eyes.

"Two in this household," Serena said proudly.

Both women heard a car pull up in front of the house, then an angry young voice. "You're lying! Leave me alone!"

The car door slammed, and Serena and Blythe looked at each other. "Sounds like Jenny's home," Blythe said.

six

Before Serena could get up to go see what had happened, Jenny came walking around the side of the house. Her head was tilted forward, as if she were deep in thought, but when she looked up, there were tears on her face.

Blythe stood up and glanced at Jenny, then back at Serena. "I think I'll go inside and see if I can help Emily."

Serena shot her a grateful glance and rose to meet her daughter. "Want to tell me about it?" she asked, rubbing a tear from Jenny's smooth cheek.

With a nod, Jenny walked over and slumped into a lounger. She stared morosely into the deep green of the garden. Serena sat quietly beside her for a moment, then asked, "Did you have another argument with Danny?"

"He's a pig!" Jenny erupted angrily.

Silently agreeing with her, Serena reached across and stroked her daughter's hair. "I've heard you say that before. What's he done this time?"

"Usual thing," Jenny mumbled. "According to him, I'm not natural because I don't want to. . .well. . .you know."

Yes, Serena knew. "You disagreed with him."

Jenny nodded. "I guess I've seen too much at Alternative." She paused. "Mom, I can forgive him for what he tried, but not for the nasty things he said when I refused." Her eyes again filled with tears and she ducked her head to hide a trembling chin.

"What did he say?"

Jenny battled silently with her tears for a moment, then sniffed and raised her head to stare back into the garden. "Can

55

I ask you something?"

"You know you can ask me anything. What is it, Honey?" Anger at Danny Scott slowly built up within Serena. Even if he was her oldest friend's son, he was a spoiled, self-centered brat who had a lot of growing up to do. Jenny was discovering that for herself.

"I was four years old when you and Daddy adopted Emily and me, right?"

Serena frowned. What did Jenny's adoption have to do with anything? "Yes, Jenny. But you know we both loved you and wanted you very much. Has Danny said something to make you doubt that?"

"No, that's not it," Jenny said quickly. "He could never do that."

Serena nodded, waiting for her to continue.

"D-did you ever meet our real mother?"

The fear stabbed more deeply through Serena before she could ward it off. After all these years, was Jenny going to try to find her real mother? "Yes, Honey, I met your natural mother twice before your daddy and I adopted you. She wanted to be sure you and Emily would have a warm, loving home."

Jenny glanced up hopefully. "Then she did care about us?"

"Very much."

"And our father? What about him?"

Serena bit her lower lip and hesitated.

"Mom?"

Serena sighed. "We never met your natural father. What little information we could discover about him led us to believe that he was too immature to shoulder the responsibilities of fatherhood." Serena knew this would not satisfy Jenny.

A quick snort of derision escaped Jenny's lips. "What took him so long? Did it take two kids for him to decide he didn't want them?"

Serena glanced across at her daughter. Maybe now was

the time to tell her, though the man's problems still didn't excuse him.

"I get the picture, Mom. Our father never wanted us in the first place. He had four whole years to learn to love me, but he must have never learned."

Serena shook her head. "Honey, your father had a lot of problems, terrible problems, and he ended up in jail for robbing a convenience store to support his drug habit."

Jenny digested this in silence, not showing the shock or horror Serena might have expected. Her mind was only on one thing—her parents' desertion.

"And our mother may have wanted us in the perfect situation, but when the times got rough, she didn't have any trouble dumping us on you."

Jenny's face crumpled, and the sight made Serena's throat swell with tears. "I don't want to hear that, Jenny," she said at last. "It was the strength of your mother's love that brought you to us. Your mother wanted you and your sister to be raised in a happy environment. She didn't have the money to support you. There was no one in her family who could help her, and she was desperate. All she wanted was for you and Emily to have a good life." Serena reached across and raised Jenny's chin, and watched her daughter's expression change as the bitterness and disillusionment faded and hope replaced it.

"Then she didn't just get tired of us and dump us with you?"

"Is that what Danny told you?"

Jenny's eyes filled back up with tears. "He said I'd better be careful about how I treat him, or he may do the same thing."

Serena hugged her daughter close. "Honey, forgive me for talking like a mother, but would it be any great loss if Danny didn't come back? You're a strong, self-confident young lady; do you think you could go solo for a while?"

Jenny swallowed and sniffed, then wiped a hand across her eyes and cocked her head to the side. "You mean dump

Danny before he has a chance to dump me?"

"Not exactly."

A faint flicker of interest showed in Jenny's eyes, and her mouth toyed with a smile. She leaned back in her chair with her hands behind her head. "Sweet revenge."

"No, that's not what I meant," Serena protested. "Even though he may act like a pig at times, he's a human being with feelings just like everyone else." Besides, right now Serena liked pigs better than she did the smart-mouthed boy who had hurt her daughter.

"You mean all guys are only interested in sex?"

"No, Honey, although it does sometimes take up a lot of their thoughts at his age. What I mean is that revenge is not for you to take. I'm not suggesting that you break up to hurt him."

"Okay, okay, Mom. Don't worry. I was just thinking about it for a minute. I couldn't really do it, you know." Jenny frowned and shook her head. "I don't know, maybe I could. Not for revenge, of course, but just to get away from the pressure for a while."

"It's up to you, Jenny. I know it would be hard, but I'll be here for you whatever you decide." She tweaked a ringlet of Jenny's dark hair, then stood up and strolled across the lawn toward the house, leaving Jenny alone to think things through.

The pungent, smoky fragrance of barbeque sauce greeted her as she stepped in the house, and she glanced through the kitchen door at Blythe and Emily.

"Do you think we could use the good china tonight?" Emily asked her grandmother.

"I think this meal deserves it," Blythe replied.

Serena slipped past and left the two talking. As she walked through the quiet house she relished the comfort of the air-conditioning. The scents of Blythe's flower arrangements drifted across from the den as she walked past it, into the bedroom, and pulled off her nearly dry bathing suit, then slumped onto the side of her bed.

"Oh, Jenny, how I wish I could do more for you," she whispered, glancing across at her older daughter's picture on top of the chest of drawers. "But you've got to make your own decisions right now. . . . I just hope you make the right ones."

She took a shower.

From somewhere in another room she heard the telephone ringing, and a few seconds later someone pounded on her bathroom door. "Mom! Hey, Mom!" Emily opened the door and traipsed into the bathroom. "Telephone. Guess who?"

Serena finished rinsing shampoo from her hair and turned off the faucets. "Hand me a towel, will you?" She held her hand over the top of the shower cubicle until Emily placed a fluffy bath towel into it.

"I'll give you a hint," Emily persisted. "He's tall, ve-ery good looking, and has the deepest, most masculine voice I've ever heard from an ER doctor."

Serena stepped out. "Hand me my bathrobe, and I'll find out for myself who this hunk is."

"Oh, come on, Mom. You know it's Carson."

"Oh, is that all?" Serena teased. "I'll have to tell him what you said about him. That should make his weekend. Thanks," she said as she took the terry robe from her daughter and pulled it on. She glanced at her bedside table, but the phone was missing. "Where's the phone?"

"Oops. I left it in the family room." Emily gave her a nervous look. "You wouldn't really tell Carson what I said!"

"Why not?" Serena led the way out of her bedroom and down the hallway to the family room. "What's wrong with letting a person know how you feel about him?"

Finally deciding her mother was teasing after all, Emily shook a reproving finger at her. "It's not nice to carry tales, you know. Besides, Carson already knows how I feel about him. Does he know how you feel?" she asked hopefully.

Serena merely grinned at her daughter as she picked up the receiver. "Hello, Carson. What can I do for you?"

"If you insist on holding such intriguing conversations with your daughter, at least hold them a little closer to the phone so I can catch every word," he complained from the other end of the line.

"You're a glutton for punishment," Serena retorted. "Don't you know eavesdroppers never hear good about themselves?"

"Yes, but at least they know where they stand. Besides, I just wanted to hear the sound of your voice again."

"I'll send you a recording," she retorted, shooing a deeply interested Emily from the room. "Better yet, why don't you just call my office number? My voice is on the answering machine."

"Should I also ask your answering machine to come to church with me in the morning?"

"Wouldn't do much good." In spite of herself, Serena could feel spirals of pleasure run through her at the warmth of his invitation.

"It doesn't hurt to try." He paused, but Serena didn't reply. "Do you have medical call next Saturday?"

She tried to remember her schedule. "I don't think so. Sally asked for weekend call this week."

"Then would you come to the lake with me?"

"I just went to the lake with you."

"Again. For the day."

"Are you kidding? A whole day away from town? I'm not sure I could handle the stress," she said dryly. "I can't remember the last time I've had the nerve to do that. What if one of my patients went into labor? What if we had a crisis at Alternative?"

"You have very competent help, and we can take a cell phone on the boat. You can be back to town in an hour if there's an emergency. Serena, give yourself a little break."

She expelled a sigh of exasperation. "You don't give up easily, do you?"

"Not when I want something badly enough."

She couldn't help it: She felt guilty, as if she were still a married woman who had just been tempted to step out on her husband. It was ridiculous, of course, but how would she be able to enjoy a day on the lake with Carson?

"No. I'm sorry," she said, and quickly changed the subject. "Have you heard from Kirby?"

"Yes." The disappointment was evident in his voice. "She'll be at your clinic Monday evening for the test results, and I hope you're there, because her parents and I will be with her."

Serena sat down abruptly as she digested this bit of information. "Her parents? She's told them?"

"Yes. I got a call from Kirby this morning during a family crisis after she told them about it. Carol's pushing for abortion, and she can push pretty hard, from what I understand."

Serena closed her eyes and sighed wearily. "What's that woman trying to do?"

"Carol is doing what so many other people do, Serena; she's hiding from the truth about Kirby's emotions and her own. She's closed her mind to it, and I haven't been able to reach her yet. We'll have a fight on our hands Monday evening, so be prepared."

"I will be, but. . .I'm glad you're going to be there."

"Well, well," he said approvingly. "That's a start."

Serena grinned. "Good-bye, Carson."

"Good-bye."

She replaced the receiver in its cradle and stepped across the thick carpeting to a window overlooking the countryside. She stared into the sky awash with gold, her mind and heart farther away than the clouds, on a tiny life she had given up so many years ago. . . .

"You and Jennings picked a good spot to build," Blythe

said from the threshold to the kitchen.

Startled, Serena jerked around to stare at her white-haired friend, then nodded. "Yes, we did, didn't we?" She glanced back out the window as Blythe crossed the room to join her. "Of course, this place was farther away from town when we first looked at it. Jeff City has spread out quite a bit since then."

"Don't worry, you're not downtown yet."

"True, but sometimes even this sprawling neighborhood makes me feel hemmed in. I guess I'll always be just a country girl at heart."

Blythe murmured agreement. One of the many things they had in common was a true love for the open country. "You never did like living in town, did you?"

"Never. I remember the day—all those years ago—when Mom and Dad decided to move to town. I cried and carried on and made life so miserable, I thought sure they'd leave me on the farm when they moved." More memories crowded in. "I had to spend my senior year of high school with strangers instead of surrounded by all my lifelong friends." Was that why she'd been so quick to accept friendship where it was offered—in the backseat of Greg Carter's parents' Buick? "I decided then that I would never do that to my own children."

Blythe grunted. "You've almost succeeded. Jenny graduates next year, and you don't act like you plan to leave before Emily does."

"No, I don't. If I show signs of doing so, you'll stop me, won't you?"

"That depends on what's most important at the time."

"There's little that's more important to a teenager." Serena slid open the silent glass doors and led the way outside. "Let's go see if we can find some salad vegetables to go with dinner."

Blythe hesitantly followed her. "I wouldn't advise it. Emily just finished chasing me out of the kitchen. I think she was afraid I'd mess up her menu." She glanced at the short terry robe Serena was wearing and raised an eyebrow. "I take it you're not going out tonight?"

"Not me." Serena inhaled, enjoying the soft fragrance of the air. "M-m-m, smell that. Are those your roses?"

Blythe grimaced. "That's our neighbor's fabric softener coming through their dryer vent."

"Oh. Sorry. I guess you and the girls are going to church in the morning as usual?"

"Of course. And, as usual, I suppose you're not?"

"Not this time." She hesitated. "Maybe soon."

"How soon? It would be so much easier for the girls if you went with us." Blythe studied Serena's closed expression. "You can't keep blaming God for Jennings's death, you know."

"I don't blame God at all." Serena shrugged. "You know how it is when you lose someone you love; you tend to stay away from the things that remind you of them the most. Maybe I just feel guilty, maybe I blame myself for his death in some way. I can't help feeling that if I'd tried harder, God wouldn't have taken him from us." She shook her head.

Blythe raised a tanned hand and touched the backs of her fingers to Serena's cheek. "Don't give me that, Serena Van Buren. Jennings's heart attack wasn't your fault, and he would not want you to blame yourself. He loved you very much. You could brighten another man's life if you only let yourself. It's what Jennings would want."

Serena chuckled, threw an arm across Blythe's shoulders, and urged her toward the house. "Not nearly as much as you brighten my life, lady."

❧

In the far, dark corner of a converted warehouse east of the city, a brown-haired, square-jawed young man named Edward stood watching his clan of workers with great pride. Most of them were teenagers, idealistic as he was, with a single focus in their hearts—to stop abortion, no matter what it took. From his informants across the city, he learned about which girls in the school system were pregnant. He tried to reach them with telephone calls, letters, or personally, before they could make the wrong decision.

He had more difficulty during the summer months than the rest of the year because there was no school to throw the kids together. But one of his workers had informed on a friend of hers, Kirby Acuff. He had put a tail on the girl and discovered some interesting information: She had visited Dr. Serena Van Buren's downtown free clinic, Alternative.

Since she was a friend of the founder's daughter, she might just have been visiting, but Edward didn't think so. Kirby Acuff liked the boys.

Edward had always had niggling doubts about this clinic called Alternative. After all, if Dr. Van Buren hated abortion as much as she pretended, she was sure low-key about it. He'd never seen her at any of the protests at the state capitol building. He intended to do more research on the whole situation. Otherwise, how could he know Dr. Van Buren wasn't an abortionist, herself?

He heard the ring of his telephone over the racket of his ancient printing press, so he reached over and jerked up the receiver. "Yes! Speak up!"

"What's that awful noise?" came Mrs. Jackson's answer to his greeting.

Edward smiled at the sound of the voice of one of his favorite teachers from high school.

"The printing press I bought last week with the money our group took in from the garage sales and bake sales this summer. I'm printing fliers for the meeting next Friday night. Did you get Serena Van Buren to speak?"

"Yes, her daughter just called. Emily also mentioned a Dr. Carson Tanner. He's an ER physician and youth leader at Serena's family's church."

"Youth leader, huh? Good. Thanks, Bev. I'll get back to you about the meeting." After hanging up, Edward returned to the printing press and turned it off. There would be time for this later. Right now, he had more investigating to do.

seven

The silence of the empty clinic weighed heavily on Serena's nerves, especially with the noisy rush-hour traffic outside the door. She glanced at her watch for the tenth time in the past half hour, then walked to the front window. The Acuffs would be off work by now, but they wouldn't have had time to get here. Out on the street, horns honked, traffic lights changed, and engines roared. Some of the storekeepers were locking up for the day, and Serena waved at a few of her acquaintances as they passed by.

She lowered the blinds. No need for every passerby to have a front row seat for the coming meeting.

She walked back to the counter and read Kirby's file once more. Test results: Positive. Just as Kirby had expected. Perhaps the coming confrontation would prompt the Acuffs to seek help for the real problem in their family—if Kirby remained strong.

A dark-haired woman about Serena's age emerged from the back of the clinic, jingling a set of keys. "All locked up, Serena. Are you sure you don't want me to stay for moral support?"

Serena shook her head. "Thanks anyway, Sharon, but Carson Tanner is coming, too. I don't want the Acuffs to feel as if we're ganging up on them."

Sharon waved. "Just call if you need anything tonight or tomorrow." She stepped out and practically collided with Kirby, who was coming in.

Serena looked at the girl in surprise. "Kirby, I didn't think you'd be here so early. I thought your parents were coming with you."

The pretty blond stepped inside. Her face was pale, and dark circles deepened her eyes. "H-hello Serena." She glanced around the big office, then stared at the entrance to the conference room. "I was supposed to wait for them, but. . .I wanted to talk to you alone before they arrived. I was afraid they might try to beat me here, though. That bus seemed to stop at every corner."

"Did you want to talk about something specific, or do you need moral support?" Serena stepped toward the conference room and gestured for Kirby to join her.

"Moral support, I guess. I need it after this weekend. I know what I'm doing is right, but my mother won't listen." Her gaze strayed to the shelves along the wall. They held replicas of an unborn baby in varying stages of development. "You don't have to tell me the results of my test. I already know I'm pregnant. I feel the same way I did the last time—morning sickness and all. And I'm grounded again, just like I was last time. It seems kind of silly, doesn't it? I mean, I can't get any more pregnant." She sat down beside Serena on a comfortable sofa.

"Kirby, there are other things that can happen besides pregnancy. I know your mother wants to do the right thing for you. What we need to do is prove to her that there's a living soul inside you, and that may be difficult to do." Serena studied the tension in the lines of Kirby's face. Would she be strong enough to oppose her angry mother? "To accept that," she continued gently, "your mother will have to accept what she's already done."

Kirby's chin jutted out. "But I accepted it, and I was the one who had the abortion." A tone of resentment entered her voice. "Mother acts as if she's the only one who's suffering. She acts like this is her life that's ruined, not mine. I made a telephone call today while they were both at work, and I found out all I have to do is go through some legal stuff and declare myself an emancipated minor. Mother can call all the police she wants, but she can't stop me. The police won't do a thing."

Serena hesitated. If Kirby did that, it might cause a damaging rift more permanent than the one they had now. Serena didn't want to undermine Carol Acuff's motherhood, but Kirby needed support. "This may be painful, and I want you to know before the meeting starts that my home is open if you need a place to stay, or if you and your parents need a few days to cool off and make some adjustments."

Kirby's eyes widened in surprise. "You'd do that?"

Serena smiled. "It isn't as if you're a stranger to us, Kirby. You've always been welcome in our home. As a guest of Jenny's, of course, you'd be treated like another one of my girls, with all the responsibilities and rules that go with it."

Kirby was thoughtful for a moment, then she shook her head doubtfully. "Mother would go nuts if I moved in with you. I think she'd rather see me try to move into my own apartment and starve to death."

The front door squeaked open, and Kirby stiffened. She and Serena turned to see Carson walk in. He wore blue scrubs and running shoes, so he must have driven straight from work. He looked tired, but when he saw Serena and Kirby, his face lit with a warm smile. "There you are. I was afraid I'd be late. We had a rush of traffic accidents thirty minutes before my shift was over, and I couldn't leave. Kirby, where are your parents?"

"Not here yet." The tension was back in her voice. She turned back to Serena. "I'm scared."

"There's nothing to be afraid of, Honey."

"How about a prayer?" Carson said softly. "I'm a little nervous, myself. I'm sure Carol and Hal will be, too."

"Better do it now, before they get here," Kirby said.

They bowed their heads, and Carson offered a simple prayer, asking for God's guidance.

Serena felt the peace of his words flow over her, and her own tension eased. It had been so long since she'd had the courage to ask God for something, but this time, in this situation, she knew it would be His will for Kirby to have this baby.

When Hal and Carol walked through the front door a few minutes later, their faces revealed the tension that was palpable in the conference room. "We're not staying long," Carol warned. "Just give the results of the test."

"I'm pregnant, okay?" Kirby snapped, her voice once again with that thread of discontent running through it, so much like her mother's.

Hal Acuff expelled a heavy sigh and looked sadly at his daughter. "Why, Kirby? Didn't you learn your lesson the first time?"

Kirby bowed her head and clasped her hands tightly together.

"What Kirby needs now is understanding." Carson looked from Hal Acuff to his wife. "She needs you to help her through this pregnancy and help her with decisions about adoption."

"No way." Carol's blue eyes grew cool. She studied her daughter's bowed head. "Kirby, do you want all of your classmates to see you waddle to classes during your senior year of high school? Is that the memory you want? Do you want them whispering and laughing behind your back?"

"I don't care what they say about me," Kirby muttered. "I can't take this baby's life."

"There's not going to be a baby."

"There already is one!" Kirby snapped. "You won't listen! You never listen."

Serena stood up and walked across to one replica on a shelf. She carried it over and held it out for them to see. "Kirby's in her second month. See the tiny baby in this piece of plastic? This is what your grandchild looks like right now. Its sex has already been determined. Its brain waves can already be recorded, and its teeth have already begun to form in the gums." She held it up so Carol could see it better. "It's a beautiful, miniature baby. That's fact, not fiction. I'm not making this up."

Carol stared at the tiny statue for a full five seconds, as if mesmerized. Her brows drew together. She pushed the statue aside and stood. "Why are you people doing this to us?" She walked to the end of the room and swung back. "Why us? Why are you picking on—"

"We're not picking on you, Carol," Carson said calmly. "We want to help you. Please just listen for a moment. We're trying to show you why Kirby threatened to take her own life the other night. We're trying to keep anything like that from happening."

Carol started to speak, swallowed, took a shaky breath, then apparently caught the compassion in Carson's eyes. She sat down on the edge of a hard-backed chair.

He continued, "Kirby can't emotionally handle another abortion, Carol. If she's forced to take this baby's life, I can't predict what will happen to her. We can save them both." He took the piece of plastic from Serena and placed it on the shelf, then turned back to Carol.

Carol glanced at Serena. Doubt entered her eyes for just a moment, then was gone. She slowly shook her head. "No." She looked down at her own hands. "Kirby can't do it."

"But it's not your decision, Mother," Kirby said. Her voice trembled, but the resolve of her words showed in her expression and the strong line of her chin. "If you don't want to help me, then I will move out."

Carol's eyes narrowed. "You're still a minor."

"I'm a pregnant minor. I have every legal right to protect this baby, and I will." Her own eyes narrowed at her mother, and for a moment their gazes did battle in silence.

"You don't have any money," Carol said at last. "You have no place to live—and don't get some crazy idea that I'll help you out."

Kirby swallowed and looked down at her nervously twisting

hands. "I'll stay with Serena."

There was a long, shocked silence, then Carol exhaled as if she'd been kicked. Growing pain and anger tightened her facial muscles as she swung on Serena. "What are you doing?" she demanded. "I can't believe you people! Now you're trying to steal my daughter!"

"I'm not—"

"Stop it!" Kirby cried. "Mother, I'm not yours to steal. I want you and Dad to leave! I'm not coming with you."

There was another shocked silence so filled with anguish, Serena couldn't bear to look into Carol's eyes.

Carson cleared his throat. "Won't you both sit back down—"

"Fine!" Carol snapped. "Stay here. Go live with your precious Serena!" Tears sprang to her eyes, and she dashed them away with the back of her hand.

A frown spread across Hal Acuff's face. "No, Kirby's our daughter. We can't just—"

"She doesn't need us." His wife's voice shook as she glared at Serena. "Are you happy?"

"I'm not happy at all, Carol," Serena said. "But Kirby has made the decision to carry this baby to term. That's what we'll help her do."

Carol turned to her daughter, her face pasty white. Her hands shook, and her voice carried a sense of betrayal. "It's as if I'm not even your mother anymore. Well, that's fine with me! You've made your choice." She took a deep breath, straightened, and turned away. "Don't bother to come by and get your things. I paid for them, I'm keeping them. Let your new mother pay your way." Without looking at Serena again, she stormed out of the clinic.

Hal watched her leave, his face as pale as Carol's. He turned to Kirby, hands spread helplessly. "She doesn't mean it, Kirby. She's just. . .can't you just do—"

"No!" She put her hands over her face. "Just go," she said

softly. "Go on with Mother. Maybe for once you can talk some sense into her."

"But I can't just leave you alone like this."

"I'm not alone." Kirby glanced hesitantly at Serena, then back to her father.

Hal shrugged and stepped forward to kiss his daughter's forehead. "You sure you'll be okay?"

"She'll be fine, Hal," Serena assured him. "She can stay with my family as long as she needs to."

He spread his hands again. "Then maybe I'd better go see if I can undo some damage."

Tears filled Kirby's eyes and trickled down her face as she watched her father walk out of the clinic in her mother's wake. "Oh, Serena, what have I done?"

Serena stood up and pulled the girl's unresisting form close and held her. She looked over the bright blond head to Carson, whose expression was sympathetic and whose physical presence lent her strength.

She gently tugged on Kirby's chin until the girl looked up at her. "Your mother's a troubled woman, and she needs our understanding and patience right now. I can't imagine how I'd feel if one of my daughters decided they wanted to live with someone else. Give her time to adjust. Maybe she'll come around."

Carson stood up. "I don't know about you two, but I could do with a nice, hot meal. Will you join me? My treat."

Kirby shook her head. "If it's okay with you, I'd just like to lie down. I'm so tired. I could rest right here on one of the beds in back while you—"

"Nonsense," Serena said. "My family is already fixing food. You can both come with me. I'll call home and tell them to set two more places, then Kirby and I can go shopping for a few necessities before we meet back at my house in. . .say. . . an hour?"

Carson inclined his head in agreement as the three of them

walked together toward the front of the clinic. Serena and Kirby stopped at a shopping center for some supplies for Kirby.

On the way to Serena's, Kirby relaxed and started talking. "Mother has her temper tantrums, but she's never been as bad as this before."

"Not even the last time you were pregnant?"

"Nope, because I did what she told me last time. But she never trusted me again. She grounded me for a whole school quarter and wouldn't even let me go to a movie or a ball game with my friends, just church. And then she even put a stop to that." Kirby looked out the side window at the passing scenery. "I'm so glad Carson didn't give up on us. He's so. . .I don't know. . .kind. He's genuine, you know? He really does care about us, and even Mom picked up on that."

She stared out the window in silence for a moment, then said, "I'm not as afraid now. Now that I know I don't have to have an abortion, there's something inside me that feels so. . . safe. Something about it feels right. I know I blew it big time, but if I ended another life to cover up what I did, I. . .couldn't live with it."

Serena reached out and touched Kirby's shoulder. "I'll be here for you. Whatever it takes."

❧

Edward drove from his parking spot near Alternative with a smile on his face. He couldn't help feeling pleased with himself. Within a forty-eight-hour period, he had discovered a lot of interesting things about Kirby Acuff. He had used acquaintances to find out information for himself and now knew Kirby's address, her telephone number, what school she attended. A friend of his who was a computer expert could find out more about Kirby's past in a couple of days. School records were next. All Edward had to do was hang around and listen a little more.

It wasn't just luck and perseverance that had put him outside

Alternative at the right time to see the Acuffs enter the building, then see the parents leave later without their daughter. He shouldn't have tried to question them, though. That mother could be vicious, and he'd had trouble judging between the truth and her distorted picture of Serena Van Buren. To hear Kirby's mother tell it, Alternative was not a pro-life clinic, but a place where Serena played out her own little God fantasies. He wouldn't make a decision about that until he knew more. Still, talking to Mrs. Acuff gave him a feel for the story he intended to write.

He knew he was definitely onto something good when he saw Kirby leave in Serena's van, and he knew God had a hand in it. Still, Edward needed more. He wanted to know more about Serena, yet she might balk at an interview, especially if any of Mrs. Acuff's bitter accusations were true.

Edward knew his methods were often questioned, but wasn't that just another sacrifice he had to make for the cause? He was willing. He didn't care what the whole world thought of him, as long as he carried out the plan.

❧

Serena was proud of her family that night. Blythe had cooked one of her special recipes with veal and rice, and Jenny, when she heard they were having company, made her homemade blueberry ice cream. Emily met Serena and Kirby at the front door and grabbed Kirby in a hug, chattering incessantly. She escorted the older girl down the hallway to the room that would be hers.

"Hi, Mom," Jenny called from the kitchen doorway. "Is she here yet?"

Serena chuckled and pointed down the hall. "Your sister's already stolen her away. Go on back and welcome her."

"You mean you let Emily take her over already? Not fair! Emily!" she called as she followed in the wake of the other two girls.

With a soft smile on her lips, Serena stood listening to the friendly, muted voices of the girls in Kirby's room. The doorbell made her jump. Carson was here already. She stepped to the door, then hesitated with her hand on the knob for a moment before she braced herself and swung it open on Carson's tall form.

"Come in," she invited. Her gaze traveled swiftly down a casual, open-necked, red knit shirt and blue jeans, then moved back up to meet his eyes. They were watching her with undisguised admiration.

He stepped into the cool interior of the house from the heat outside. "You did well tonight. How's your guest doing?"

"The girls have taken her over. I think she'll be fine for now. I feel awful about Carol. I know she must be devastated."

"But I'm sure you understand this is necessary."

"Yes, but it's still painful." Serena led him into the family room where Rascal lay sprawled across the sofa in an attitude of dejection.

"What's the matter, boy, did they run you out of the kitchen?" She reached down and scratched his ears.

"Need any help with the food?" Carson asked.

"Are you kidding? In this houseful of cooks? I'll just go check on things and call you when it's ready."

Dinner turned out to be as good as Serena had expected, and she was gratified to discover that Kirby had shed the last of her misgivings and relaxed as if she were already a part of the family. Whenever the girl's face grew sober, Emily poked her from one side or Jenny whispered to her from the other, and the melancholy disappeared.

After an hour of talk, laughter, delicious food, and reprimanding Rascal-the-beggar under the table, Carson laid down his napkin and stood up. "That was a wonderful meal. Thank you for inviting me. I'd stay and help with the cleanup, but there are a few loose ends I need to tidy before I call it a night." He bent toward Serena. "I think Kirby will be just fine with the four of you. Want to walk me to my car? I could use a consult."

The sky was still bright when they stepped out the front door, and Serena felt a cool mist touch her face as a gentle breeze carried a spray from the sprinkler system in the neighbor's lawn. The fragrance of pine perfumed the air, and Carson inhaled appreciatively.

"I envy you, Serena. I wish I had an evergreen forest in my front yard." He chuckled. "I wish I had a front yard."

"That's a difficult thing to come by in a high-rise apartment, isn't it?"

"Very," he agreed. "But then, what's a pine forest or a nice house in the country without someone to share it with? An apartment building at least gives the impression of company."

"I'm sure you're right. This place would get pretty lonely without the others. I never lived alone. Is it difficult?"

Carson opened his car door and turned to look at Serena. "Very. It isn't so bad until you find someone you want to spend your time with—then, it's very lonely."

Serena looked away.

"Don't get too attached to Kirby," Carson said.

Serena glanced back at him. "I'm already attached. Are you going to try to talk to her parents again?"

He nodded. "Neither she nor the baby needs the added pressure of her estrangement from her parents. As you said, Carol Acuff has problems of her own, but I think tonight might precipitate a change. You handled the situation very well."

"Kirby did most of it."

"Without your support, she may not have had the courage to do it," Carson replied. He touched her cheek in a tender caress.

The warmth of that touch sent a quick tingle of pleasure through her.

"You impress me, Serena."

"That just proves how little you actually know about me."

He got into his car and started the quiet engine. "Then I think it's time I got to know you better," he replied softly, then raised his hand in a half salute and backed out of the driveway.

With a feeling of bemusement, Serena watched until he turned a corner and disappeared from sight behind a stand of pine trees. The thing she had never expected to happen again was happening. If she weren't careful, she could easily fall in love with Carson Tanner.

&

The minute Carson stepped into his apartment, he switched on his desk lamp and sat down. There were three things he had to do before he went to bed tonight. First, he made a note to transfer funds to his checking account and write a sizable check to Alternative next week. He had always believed in what Serena was doing there, but after tonight, he felt a strong conviction to help her in every way he could. She was saving lives. This time, his donation wouldn't be anonymous.

He reached for the telephone. He had already memorized the Acuffs' number. He dialed it and waited. It rang eight times before he hung up. Where were they? He'd have thought Carol would grab the phone at first ring, if she was there. If she wasn't there, where would she be? Barging in at Serena's to drag her daughter home?

He had seen the pain in Carol's eyes several times tonight, and in Hal's. If he could do nothing else, he might be able to ease some of that pain until they grew strong enough to see the truth for themselves: No one would take their place in the heart of their daughter.

He dialed Serena's number. Was he calling too late? Apparently not, for someone answered on the second ring. "Hello?" It was Emily's voice, and Carson smiled to himself at the sweet sound.

"Are the dinner dishes all washed?"

"Hi, Carson! Yes, the kitchen's spotless. Do you want to talk to Mom?"

"That would be nice."

"Okay, but first I want to ask you a favor, but promise not to say anything to Mom." She didn't wait for him to reply. "Would you be interested in talking in an open forum next Friday night at a school board meeting? It's about teenage pregnancy."

He glanced at his calendar. He was free. "I'd love to."

"Good, because I promised Mrs. Jackson I'd probably be able to get you. I'll get Mom now and give you the details later."

Serena sounded tired when she came on the phone, and Carson took pity on her. "I won't keep you long, I just wanted to see how Kirby was settling in." *And to hear your voice again.*

"She's doing very well."

"Good. You wouldn't have, by chance, changed your mind about going to church, would you? We could use some extra prayers right now."

"No, Carson, I haven't. But thank you. You'll have to pray extra for me."

"I have been praying for you, Serena."

"That wasn't what I—"

"Are you trying to tell me how to pray?" Carson asked gently.

Serena hesitated. "No. I just feel that Kirby needs prayer more than I do right now."

"Maybe not. Good night, Serena. I'll be seeing you soon."

eight

As the summer advanced into August, Serena's patients complained about the heat. Blythe predicted the drought would kill her garden. Serena felt the familiar weight of depression drag her down as the calendar advanced. It was always the same. This time of the year was the most difficult for her and had been for all of her adult life.

Kirby settled into the household comfortably, but Serena often saw the sadness in the girl's eyes. For the first two nights, after Jenny and Emily went to bed, Kirby sat up and stared silently out of the bay window in the family room. Serena and Blythe, sensing that she needed time alone to adjust, stayed nearby, but they didn't pester her with questions or idle chatter.

Wednesday night, Serena sat down beside the pretty teenager on the sofa. "Can't sleep?"

Kirby shook her head.

"Want to talk about it?"

Tears filled Kirby's eyes, and she sniffed. "I feel so guilty for hurting my mother."

"That's natural," Serena assured her. "But you know what you're doing is the right thing. We need to give your mother time to realize that." She couldn't help wondering if Carson had spoken with Carol.

They sat in silence for a few moments, listening to the ticking of the grandfather clock. Blythe was in the kitchen baking a batch of cookies, humming a familiar gospel tune, and the sounds she made were homey, familiar, comforting—at least to Serena. She hoped they were to Kirby.

"It was nice to go to the youth meeting with Jenny tonight," Kirby said at last. "A bunch of the kids got together for pizza afterwards, and it felt good just to sit and talk about stuff. I've really missed that." She paused and glanced at Serena. "On the way home, Jenny told me again how she feels about God."

Serena kicked off her sandals and tucked her feet underneath her. "Jenny has strong Christian convictions."

"Yeah, I know. She always has, but I guess this time I listened better. She. . .told me that God can forgive me for my abortion, if I will only ask Him."

Serena nodded. "Did you ask Him?

"N–no."

"Don't you believe He'll forgive you?"

"I. . .don't know. Maybe I don't know God well enough yet, or maybe I don't think I deserve to be forgiven."

"Don't you think you should let God be the judge of that?" Jenny should be in here talking to Kirby. Serena felt suddenly incompetent.

Kirby got up and stretched. "Maybe I'll go to church with Jenny on Sunday. Although now Mother says anyone who goes to church and calls himself a Christian is just a hypocrite."

After telling Kirby good night, Serena stretched out on the sofa and stared outside. She didn't go to church, avoided talking to God, and avoided talking about Him; and yet, when someone asked, she called herself a Christian. Was she a hypocrite?

❧

Thursday morning Carson dialed the Acuff number. He had done so every morning and night since Kirby went to stay with Serena. He expected the same results as before—an answering machine, but this time Hal picked up.

"I was beginning to think you'd gone out of town," Carson said after he identified himself.

"We did, Carson. We went to stay with Carol's sister in St. Louis for a couple of days. Carol's pretty upset about all this.

Kirby's okay, isn't she?"

"I was hoping you would call her and see." Carson tried to keep the sharpness from his voice.

"I would have. It's just that. . .well. . .Carol already thinks we're ganging up on her. I thought if Kirby called her first. . ."

"Your daughter's feelings are important here, too."

"I know they are, and I promise I'll call her as soon as I get a break this morning at work." Hal lowered his voice. "Carol's back in the bedroom getting dressed. She's more upset than I've ever seen her. She's cried every day since Kirby left. She blames Serena Van Buren."

In Carson's opinion, which he kept to himself, Carol was always eager to blame somebody besides herself, but that wasn't the compassionate Carson talking.

"Carol loves Kirby," Hal continued. "She just likes to be in charge, and when Kirby doesn't do what Carol wants, it upsets her. Kirby has her mother's stubborn streak, and so she rebels. It's my fault as much as Carol's."

"Have you tried telling your wife how you feel?"

"I've tried. . .but—"

"It might be what she needs to hear, Hal."

"Do you know how long things have gone on like this? We've fallen into a routine."

"Is the routine working?" Carson asked.

"No."

"I'd like to try to help you. We could set up some meetings with Kirby when the three of you feel you can handle it emotionally."

There was a pause.

"Will you think about it?"

Hal hesitated. "Yeah, I'll think about it."

❧

Kirby was still asleep when the Van Burens finished breakfast Thursday morning, and at Serena's request, Emily and Blythe took pains to be quiet while they did the dishes. Jenny didn't have to be at work until ten this morning, but she got ready early so she could ride to town with her mother.

"Why did you decide to go with me instead of letting Granny take you later?" Serena asked Jenny as they climbed into the van. "You know you'll have to wait around for two hours until the shops open."

"I want to talk to you alone, Mom," Jenny replied. "You have been so busy lately. It seems like you're never around anymore."

Serena glanced at her daughter in dismay. "I'm sorry."

"Mom, has something been bothering you?" Jenny asked.

Serena stopped in the process of buckling her seat belt. "What?"

Jenny shrugged. "You've been so. . .so quiet. And you've been going to work real early. Why?"

Serena looked into her daughter's questioning eyes for a brief moment, then sighed. It wasn't something she could talk about with her family. "I guess I just get so busy, I forget to take time for the most important people in my life sometimes." Serena rolled down the window and inhaled the fresh morning air. "I'm sorry, Honey. I'll try to do better."

"Don't work yourself to death, Mom. We need you. You can't take on the whole world."

Serena patted her daughter's knee and backed out into the street. "I'll remember that. Now, tell me what's on your mind."

Jenny sat back in her seat. "I took your advice. I broke up with Danny a couple of days ago. I would've told you sooner, but with all the stuff going on with Kirby, I decided it could wait."

Serena felt an immediate lifting of her spirits. No more worrying whether or not Danny would break down Jenny's will. "How did it go?"

Jenny grimaced. "Not exactly like I'd expected. Mom, he

almost cried! I felt so bad. But I didn't let him talk me out of it, as hard as he tried."

"Are you sorry you did it?" Serena asked as they merged with the heavier city traffic and stopped at the first signal.

Jenny hesitated. "I don't know yet. I know I miss him. And I keep wondering if he'll go out with other girls."

"How will you feel if he does?"

"How do you think? Awful! But maybe he won't. He. . .he said he loved me and that if I didn't think we should go all the way, he could wait, if only I wouldn't break up with him. I just hope. . .I hope. . .oh, I don't know. . .I feel so lonely now without him. I hope I find out that he's sincere, but if he isn't, then it wasn't God's will for us to be together." She paused and stared out the window for a moment. "And there's something else, Mom."

"What's that?"

"Danny isn't a Christian. I mean, he says he is, and he's gone to a lot of the youth activities at church; but he doesn't actually live it, you know? If he did, he wouldn't be pressuring me like he is."

"And how do you feel about that?"

"I feel like there's something missing. It's like there's a whole section of my life I can't share with him, and it's the most important section."

Serena glanced sharply at her daughter. *The most important section.* "Jenny, you and I don't. . .talk about God very often, either, since your father died."

Jenny continued to stare out the window. "I know."

The words sank deeply into Serena's heart. She completed the drive downtown in thoughtful silence. Jennings had been on her mind since she'd awakened this morning, and her sense of loss had been keen. His love had helped her forget the harshness of her past and healed some of her brokenness. Not all of it, but enough to face life. He hadn't ever known the depth of her pain, and she'd hidden it well, but his gentleness and joy lightened the burden she carried. When he died, she lost the peace he had brought into her world. She had placed so much of her faith in her husband, in his encouragement, support, and love. When she lost it, she felt as if she'd lost everything.

When they drove past Alternative, Jenny said quickly, "Stop here, Mom, and I'll open up this morning. Sharon will be here before I have to go to work, won't she?" The girl glanced along the street in both directions and opened her van door. "At least that man isn't hanging around today."

Serena shot her daughter a sharp look. "What man? What are you talking about?"

Jenny shrugged. "Probably nothing. I saw some guy hanging around the sidewalk a couple of times, and it looked to me like he was watching the clinic. Maybe I was just paranoid."

"I'm not sure I like the sound of this. What did he look like?"

Jenny shrugged. "I knew I shouldn't have told you. He didn't look bad. He was clean and friendly looking. He talked to one of the volunteers—I think it was Karen—when she left to go home the other afternoon."

"You mean he stopped her on the sidewalk?" Serena had trouble controlling the anxiety in her voice.

"Yeah, but she talked to him for a few minutes—I know, because I watched to make sure he wasn't bothering her—and she never acted upset. She was still smiling when she said goodbye to him. He's probably just taking a poll or something."

"Did he have a clipboard?"

Jenny frowned. "I can't remember. I'll watch for him today and see."

"You'll do it this afternoon, then. I'm not leaving you here alone this morning."

"Oh, Mom!"

"Close your door." Serena put the van in gear and pulled

away from the curb. "You can wait at my office or where you work. It makes no difference to me, but I'm not taking any chances. I want to find out what that man wanted."

ಜ

Serena called Karen Parker as soon as the first patient left her office, but learned only that the strange man was polite, soft spoken, and interested in the activities of the clinic. He had apparently known what Alternative's function was and seemed enthusiastic about it. He didn't sound threatening. Still, Serena wished she knew more about him.

After the third patient left that morning, Gail came into the office with the mail, laid it on Serena's desk, and proceeded to the sink for the watering can.

Busy with an information sheet on a new patient, Serena shuffled through the pile quickly, her mind barely registering the names on the envelopes, until she came across Carson's return address. She slit the top of the envelope and pulled out a folded sheet of paper. When she opened it, a check fell out on the desk—in the amount of ten thousand dollars.

She gasped. She closed her eyes and shook her head, then looked back at the check, sure she must have imagined it. . . but there it was, written out in Carson's unmistakable handwriting.

It was for the Alternative clinic.

She picked up the letter that had come with it. "Dr. Van Buren," it read, "until I can be more personally involved with your clinic, I hope this can be of use. I believe in you, Serena, and I believe in what you're doing. Carson."

Serena leaned back in her chair and stared, unseeing, out her office window. A soft smile spread across her face. She reached for the phone to call him, but before she could pick up the receiver, it buzzed. When she answered, there was a short silence at the other end of the line.

"Serena, this is Carol Acuff. I want to know how my daughter is."

Serena hesitated in surprise. Things were happening a little faster than she could handle. "I think she's at the house," she said at last. "Why don't you call her there and find out?"

"Not right now. She'd probably hang up on me."

"I don't—"

"Just tell me how she is," Carol demanded.

Serena relented. "Kirby is fine physically. She's eating well, and she's getting along very nicely with my daughters. If you want to know how she's feeling emotionally, call her."

"What do you want from my daughter?" Carol asked with sudden bitterness. "Why are you going so far out of your way for her?"

"You already know the answer to that," Serena said quietly.

"So what's in it for you?"

Serena bit the inside of her lower lip to keep from snapping back.

"You were the one who sicced that jerk on me the other night, weren't you?"

Serena frowned. Was the woman losing touch with reality? "Who are you talking about?"

"That guy on the street. I walked out of the clinic, and there he was—asking me what was going on in there. What was he, a reporter? What are you up to? Did you write out the sermon he preached at me? All that garbage about abortion murdering babies. There isn't any baby, and you can't kill something that hasn't started living!"

Serena could feel the heat of her anger flushing her face. "Were you with Kirby through the abortion she had two years ago, Carol? Did you see them do the procedure?"

"Of course not."

"Then don't tell me it wasn't already a baby. Maybe if you'd been there for her—"

Serena broke off, appalled at what she was doing, what she was saying. The sound of a quiet sob snapped her attention back to the telephone. "Carol, are you still there?"

"It wasn't a baby," the woman said softly.

"Just keep telling yourself that," Serena said. "But while you're doing that, why don't you ask yourself where you would be now if your parents had opted for an abortion. Where would Kirby be?"

There was a swift intake of breath and then a snap as the line disconnected, and Serena felt a cold wash of shock at the harshness of her own words.

nine

Thursday afternoon brought a light, refreshing shower, and its effect was not only cooler temperatures, but cooler tempers. The tension that settled into Serena's neck muscles throughout the day disappeared. She stepped over to the window to inhale the fresh scent of rain and gazed with pride at the tree-lined streets and hills of Jefferson City. From where she stood, she could see the huge, white dome of the capitol building where it overlooked the sparkling Missouri River. The city spread over rolling hills, presenting an image of peace. If Serena had her choice of all the cities and towns in the country in which to work and raise a family, she would still have chosen Jeff City.

"Good night, Gail," she called as she locked her office door and walked across the carpeted floor of the outer office. "Is your car still running, or do you need a ride home?"

"Running fine, but I'll go down with you anyway. I had a call today that might interest you." Gail turned off her computer and grabbed her purse as she stood to leave.

"A call? What kind of a call?"

Gail took out a ring of keys to lock the door, and their noisy jingle echoed through the empty corridor. "It seemed like just a request for information, but it was a pretty detailed request. Some man—he sounded young—wanted to know how many girls you saw at Alternative. He wanted to know how many volunteers you had working for you and what their names and addresses were."

"You didn't tell him, did you?"

"Of course not."

Serena pressed the elevator button. "Jenny told me about a man who's been hanging around outside the clinic." The elevator slid open, and Gail preceded Serena inside.

"What did he look like?" Gail asked.

"Young, slender, brown hair. He had the nerve to talk to one of my volunteers and to Carol Acuff."

"Maybe he's harmless."

"Or maybe not. What else did he ask you?"

"He flat out asked me if you ever arranged for abortions through the clinic."

Serena stifled a gasp. "What did you tell him?"

"At first I didn't say anything, he surprised me so. I thought surely he'd at least know that much about Alternative if he was really interested—though I can't imagine why, unless he has a girlfriend or sister or somebody close to him who's pregnant. But you know what, Serena? I don't know if he believed me. He sounded really sarcastic when he asked me if I was sure about the abortions."

"If he ever calls again, give him to me. I want to have a little talk with this young man."

They stepped out of the elevator and through the revolving glass doors into the newly cooled, rain-washed air and walked toward the parking lot.

"He asked something else, too," Gail said. "He asked if Kirby Acuff was a patient here."

"And?"

"I guess I got a little huffy with him. Instead of just telling him we didn't give out that information, I told him it was none of his business and, if he wanted to waste any more of our time, he would have to make an appointment and talk to you."

"Good. Maybe you scared him off." Serena doubted it, but she could hope. This guy was beginning to worry her.

⁂

The telephone was ringing when Serena walked into the house an hour later, and she frowned as she rushed into the family room to answer it. Where was everybody?

A glance out into the backyard gave her the answer. Blythe was in the garden, and Jenny and Kirby were barbequing steaks on the grill by the patio. As Serena lifted the receiver to her mouth, she caught a glimpse of Emily dashing out from the side of the house, with Rascal tripping her up at every step. "Hello."

"Hello, Serena."

It was Carson's deep voice, and Serena couldn't control the leap of pleasure she felt. "Carson! I tried calling you today."

"Oh? If you'd called your clinic, you would have found me. I had some time and thought I might be of some use there."

"And were you?"

"You'll have to ask Sharon. I'm afraid I asked more questions than anything else, but I did learn a lot. Why did you try to call me? Is something wrong with Kirby?"

"No, I wanted to thank you for the check; but now that I have you on the line, I don't know what to say. How can I thank you?"

"I didn't do it for thanks, I wanted to invest in a good thing."

"Thank you, Carson."

"You're welcome. What I called you about was a date, but now it's going to sound as if I'm trying to buy one with you, and I'm not. Would you come out for a drive with me tonight?"

"But then you might think I was only going with you because of the money."

He laughed. "I knew that would cause problems. Come with me anyway."

"I'll tell you what: The girls are barbequing steaks outside right now. Would you like to come over?"

"I will if you'll come for a drive with me afterward."

Serena smiled. "Okay. If a noisy dinner here with my family and a quiet drive afterwards will make up for the ten thousand dollars, then far be it from me to question your sanity."

"Why don't you try to figure it out for yourself? I'll see you soon." Without waiting for an answer, he hung up.

At Blythe's suggestion, the girls set up the table in the backyard. It was seldom cool enough to have a picnic this time of year, and they intended to take full advantage of the weather. Even Rascal sensed the party atmosphere and made a nuisance of himself as he dashed and played around their feet.

After a quick shower, Serena pulled on a pair of black denim jeans and a crocheted turquoise blouse. She cast a doubtful glance in her closet at her five pairs of sandals, then decided she would be more comfortable barefoot—she was always more comfortable barefoot.

The sound of a closing car door alerted her to Carson's arrival just before the doorbell chimes echoed through the house, and Serena felt the quickening of her breath. She glanced at the mirror one more time, gave her hair a final shake, and headed down the hallway to greet him. Her heart pounded loudly in her chest, and she pressed a damp palm against the denim material of her jeans as she swung the door open on its hinges.

What she saw sent her eyes widening in appreciation and her lips answering his broad smile of greeting. Her glance traveled slowly and appreciatively up his casual look. He wore black denim shorts and a white "Christ First" T-shirt. Her eyes traveled on up, only to rest on a frankly amused face. "You did say barbeque. . .?"

"Sure did, and you look great." She turned to lead him out toward the back patio. "Are you hungry? The girls really got involved in their cooking today." She kept her eyes away from his and concentrated on breathing evenly, all too aware of his disturbing presence directly behind her. Tonight, more than ever, she felt his quiet magnetism.

The smoky aroma of sizzling steaks made Serena's mouth water when she led the way out of the house, and she eyed a large platter of them hungrily. Jenny—or perhaps Kirby—had been generous with Blythe's special barbeque sauce, and Emily had tossed a magnificent green salad of crisp vegetables from the garden. Blythe had spread a large, red checked cloth over the long picnic table and was setting it with their finest china and silver. Serena raised a questioning brow when she noted their best crystal glasses set incongruously against the background of red and white checks.

"For a barbeque?" she asked Blythe under cover of the teenagers' loud welcome to Carson. "What is this, a celebration?"

Blythe glanced up from where she folded linen napkins. "Nope. No celebration, just good company." She glanced approvingly at Carson.

"Okay, everybody," Emily said, "it's ready. Come on, I'm starved!"

Carson asked the blessing for the food, and Serena's heart was touched by the simple sincerity of his words. He asked God to help Kirby become reunited with her family, and tears pricked Serena's eyes. She fought them furiously, unwilling for the others to see how sensitive she was just now. A beautifully grilled steak, thick with browned sauce, plopped onto her plate, and she jerked up to find Carson smiling at her.

"Join the party, Serena."

She returned his smile, picked up a fork and steak knife, and cut her T-bone into bite-sized pieces. She spooned out a large helping of Emily's crunchy salad, complete with creamy buttermilk dressing and sunflower seeds. Emily was proud of this salad recipe. It was one she had invented herself, and she'd even won an award in a contest at the fair last year.

Jenny leaned across the table with a small bowl. "Mom,

dunk your cherry tomatoes in this sweet and sour sauce. . .and here, did you taste this corn on the cob? We roasted it on the grill with the steaks."

The low hum of talk at the table quickly grew to confused chatter, and Serena sat in silence, her glance roving from one face to the next. Blythe discussed a new recipe for homemade ice cream with Jenny, occasionally calling a warning at Rascal, who yapped for a handout. Carson joined in the conversation, surprising Emily and Jenny with his knowledge of cooking.

Blythe leaned toward Serena, her expression suddenly sober. "Have you had any phone calls from a member of the Save-a-Life group?"

"Never heard of them. Who are they?"

Blythe took a sip of her fruit punch. "That's what I wanted to know when some guy called here this morning looking for you. Now, don't get excited, but I got curious enough to attend one of their meetings today."

"Sounds harmless enough. What happened?"

Blythe lowered her voice. "Kind of weird, if you ask me. Scary, even. This guy named Edward—didn't give a last name —seemed to run the thing. He led all kinds of chants against abortion. Some of it even sounded violent. They hate abortion, that's for sure, but they don't show much compassion. They were all pretty young. . .in their late teens, early twenties. The guy talked about God a lot, but I never heard him actually pray."

Serena thought about the man Jenny had mentioned hanging around the clinic and talking to Karen, who had accosted Carol Acuff and called Gail. "Did he say why he was trying to call me?"

"He heard about Alternative and thought you might be interested in joining their group."

"Did you set him straight?"

"Tried to. I told him you went about things peacefully, but

he gave me some speech about banding together to get things done. They're talking about another meeting Friday night. I think I'll go again."

Serena set down her glass and stared at Blythe.

"Now, don't worry," Blythe assured her. "I'm not getting crazy on you, but I'm curious. I'd like to know what they're up to. Ever heard of a mob mentality?"

"Of course."

"That's what this is. I met some people there today who seemed like decent folks until Edward got them all excited about 'the killers paying for their sins.' "

"And you're going back?"

"I'd feel safer knowing what's going to happen. You don't build that kind of heat in people without having a fire. I just don't trust them."

"Maybe I should go with you."

"Afraid I can't handle myself? Don't worry, these old bones have some life in them, yet. You just have to convince them you know what you're talking about, and I think I can bluff them."

Serena nodded with reluctance. Blythe would do what she wanted anyway, but she had common sense. She could handle it.

The food vanished with amazing speed, and Emily jumped up when she saw Serena finish a last bite of steak. "Don't anybody move," the girl said as she ran toward the house. "Dessert is on its way." She disappeared into the house and emerged seconds later carrying a basket made out of a watermelon rind and filled with every fresh fruit conceivable, from bananas to kiwi to oranges. Emily's golden brown eyes shone with pleasure as she placed the salad in front of Carson and earned his immediate praise.

Serena watched the obvious display of affection between Carson and her youngest daughter. Jenny and Emily needed someone like him—she needed someone like him—to share her life with, to share her love, to share some of her burdens.

She nibbled on her fruit salad and watched the way Carson talked with the rest of them. He wasn't flamboyant in any way, yet his deep, quiet voice drew their attention the same way the glowing patio lamp was drawing moths in the fading evening light.

She bit into a tart, juicy kiwi and glanced up to find Carson watching her. He laid a hand on her arm and bent near. "I seem to remember your promise of a moonlight drive after dinner."

The tingling firmness of his hand and voice seemed to penetrate into her bones, and she nodded wordlessly. She slipped out along the bench and picked up dishes and plates.

"We'll handle the dishes," Kirby insisted, her blue eyes dancing as she took the empty plates from Serena's hands.

With a helpless shrug, Serena turned to Carson. "You win," she conceded. "Just let me get my shoes."

ten

"Where are we going?" Serena asked as Carson backed onto the empty street.

"Good question."

"You don't know?"

"I don't have a clue." He shot her a teasing glance. "I just wanted to get you alone for a few minutes."

"Okay, but you're not going to take me on a moonlight hike in the woods or anything are you? I'm only wearing sandals, and—"

"No hike tonight. The copperheads will be out."

Serena buckled her seat belt and settled back. She had to be honest with herself—she liked being alone with Carson Tanner. Of course, she would never admit that to him. Probably.

He drove the car around the winding streets of the peaceful suburb and finally merged with the sparse traffic on the expressway, heading away from the city lights. Country. Yes, he knew her well.

The night sounds of cicadas reached Serena's ears in a whisper through the closed windows of the car, and she listened contentedly. It felt good just to relax beside Carson. She gazed up at him through lowered lashes and bit her lip. She couldn't stop her imagination. What would it be like to spend more time with him like this? To have this to look forward to every day when she came home from work? To share—

No. She couldn't allow herself to go there.

"Deep thoughts?" he asked.

"Not particularly. I was. . .thinking about lots of things." She turned toward him in the seat. "Have you noticed how well Kirby seems to have settled in? She gets along very well with both Emily and Jenny."

The corners of Carson's eyes creased in a smile. "Do I detect a little maternal pride?"

"Do you blame me?"

"No. You have reason to be proud of them. I'm sure their friendship has helped her through this estrangement from her parents." He glanced briefly at Serena. "Until tonight, since the girls look so much like Jennings, I didn't know they were adopted. Emily told me."

"It's no big secret; it never has been. Even if we'd tried, we couldn't have kept it a secret. Jenny was four years old when we adopted them. She vaguely remembers her mother."

"You should counsel more adoptive parents. You've done so well with Jenny and Emily."

"Thank you. I think the girls are rather proud of the fact that Jennings and I actually chose them to be our children. It makes them feel special."

Carson slowed the car and turned off the expressway. "I think being loved by you would make anyone feel special."

"Being loved makes everyone feel special," Serena replied. "And since they're so attached to Kirby, she's bound to feel better than she did before. Life is so empty when you're not loved."

From the corner of her eye, Serena could see Carson nod in agreement; but when she looked across at him, the lights from the dash showed a frown marring his straight, black brows.

The narrow country lane entered a forest, and the headlights of the car reflected back at them from heavy foliage alongside the road. "I'm wondering how Jenny and Emily will react when Kirby returns home," Carson said.

Serena glanced over in surprise. "Is she going home?"

Carson stopped the car, switched off the ignition, and leaned back in his seat. "I called and spoke with Hal this morning. He was anxious about Kirby."

"So is Carol," Serena said. "She called me this afternoon to ask about her daughter, and I blew it, big time."

"Tell me."

"Well, I'm afraid I wasn't very professional." She hesitated, glanced at him, then looked away. She recounted to him the conversation with Carol, feeling her face flush with shame. "I'm sorry. I've become too emotionally involved with this situation. It's a bad tendency I have. I do it with patients, too."

Carson gently touched her cheek, and she looked up. "You may have gotten through to her when no one else could. Maybe she needs to see a show of force. Did you tell her how Kirby was?"

"I told Carol her daughter was fine physically, but that she would have to call Kirby and ask her how she was otherwise."

"Good." Carson slid the windows down with a quiet shush, and the night sounds of the crickets and cicadas came tumbling into the car with them. "I have a feeling Kirby may go home before she has the baby. I'll see if they'll talk to us again, kind of keep the communication lines open. But Serena, I'm an ER doc, not a psychologist or family counselor."

"And I'm a hot-tempered OB/Gyn doc, but I don't think Carol Acuff would agree to professional counseling again. It didn't help before. We'll do our best to convince them to try with the counselor at Alternative. I really want them to have qualified, experienced guidance. If they refuse, it looks like they're stuck with us—if they'll let us help."

"We'll have to leave that up to God."

Serena nodded. The rich forest scents drifted through her window, and she breathed deeply. It smelled of dirt and hay and cedar. "How much longer do you think we'll get to keep Kirby?"

"It depends on Carol. It may be another week, maybe two. That is, if Kirby wants to go back home. She's pretty much in the driver's seat right now, because all she has to do is hold the 'emancipated minor' threat over their heads."

Serena hoped, for the sake of Kirby's family, that she reconciled with Hal and Carol and went back home, but a selfish voice inside argued with logic. Serena was growing more and more attached to Kirby and to the life that grew inside the young woman. How precious. How miraculous. To be a part of that. . .

"May I ask a personal question?" Carson lay an arm across the back of the seat. "Why did you adopt Jenny and Emily?"

"Because Jennings and I loved children, and. . .and we could have none of our own." She didn't feel it necessary to explain why.

"You made a good choice. I'm impressed by your girls." He paused, cleared his throat. "Sometimes I wish we had adopted. My wife and I couldn't have children, either."

"I'm sorry." Serena looked down at her twined fingers and felt a sudden emotional heaviness. "That's not an easy thing to accept. I should know. I've lived with that same knowledge since I was a teenager." She raised her eyes back up to meet his through the darkness. "Did you feel terribly deprived?"

"I did at first, but there's much more to life and love than fathering children. I believe my wife was hurt much more than I was, but when I suggested adoption, she immediately rejected the idea." He reached out to touch Serena, but drew back. "Now, seeing you with your daughters, I wish I'd tried harder to convince her to adopt. It's like you said, you seem to have a special relationship with them because you chose them. Speaking of your daughters. . .why don't you bring them and Kirby and Blythe, and come to the lake with me Saturday?"

"You already asked, remember? I declined."

"But I didn't invite your whole family. This is different. Would you consider it? You said you didn't have call."

The idea was tempting, but Serena shook her head. "No,

Blythe is supposed to spend the day with an old friend of hers, and I don't think it would be a very—"

"Why not?" he interrupted, expelling a sigh of impatience. "Serena, until you give me a good reason why I shouldn't, I'm going to keep asking you to spend time with me."

The chirruping of tiny forest dwellers grew louder in Serena's ears, and all her other senses came alive in her awareness of Carson. He sat across from her, silent, as if waiting for her to argue. The clean male scent of him was strong in her nostrils, and she felt every fiber of her body reaching out to him, but still she held back.

He shifted slightly, and her heart skipped a beat when she thought he intended to move toward her. But he didn't. He just stared questioningly at her through the darkness. Her lungs felt empty of air, and she drew a shaky breath, fully aware of the raspy sound coming from her throat.

It seemed so long since Jennings had died, so long, and she had been terribly lonely. If she could just touch Carson, just feel the strength of his arms around her one time. . . .

Of its own volition, her right hand reached across the expanse separating them. She stopped herself and drew back, but too late. Carson caught the gesture, and he grasped her hand before she could draw completely away. "No, Serena," he entreated. "Don't pull away."

He urged her closer, and incapable of resisting him, she allowed him to draw her across the soft seat into the arms she had so longed to feel around her. He drew her against his chest, and his firm lips came down on hers, and immediately she panicked and pulled back. Even in the darkness, she knew he must be able to see the pain in her eyes, so she closed them and ducked her head. "I shouldn't even be here, Carson. I still feel. . ."

"Married. I know. But you're not. Don't be afraid of intimacy, Serena. I mean emotionally, not physically. Well. . .I mean physically, too, I suppose, but. . ."

If it had been lighter in the car, Serena was sure she would have caught Carson blushing. She smiled. "I guess it's been a long time since either of us has dated."

"Yes, I guess it has. Longer for me. I'm afraid I'm extremely rusty at this, and I know that doesn't sound romantic, but the feelings are here, Serena. I could easily fall in love—"

Serena reached up and pressed her fingers gently to his lips. "No, Carson. You don't know what you're saying. You don't know me."

"Nothing I could discover about you now would change my heart."

Serena withdrew from him. "It's getting late," she said. "I have a long day tomorrow."

Carson slid back behind the steering wheel and started the engine. He glanced sideways at her. "Serena, no matter how precious Jennings was to you, he's gone and I'm here. My wife was dear to me. I loved her and supported her and protected her, but she's with the Lord now." He turned the car back toward town. "I'm more lonely since I've met you than I ever was at any other time in my life. I was ready to live alone, but when you came along, you upset all my decisions."

Serena looked across at him and laid her head against the soft headrest. "Tell me about your wife. Tell me about your past. Sometimes I think I know a person well, when in reality I know very little, because our pasts are what shape us. Where were you born and reared? How long were you married?"

Carson turned onto the expressway. "Deft change of subject. Okay, you win. I was born and raised down in the Missouri bootheel, close to the St. Francis River. Like most country boys in that area, I spent a lot of time along the river—exploring, fishing, and swimming. I went to school in a town called Kennett. I suppose that's why I like Jeff City so much, because even though this city is larger, it has the same easy, countrified atmosphere as Kennett."

Serena watched the lights of the city appear on the horizon. "Don't you ever have the urge to go back to the country? I think I would feel stifled living in an apartment."

"Yes, as a matter of fact, I do long for the country life again. That's why I bought some land down by the lake a few years ago, before Judy's death. She was a city girl and afraid to live in the country. I felt sure she would change her mind when she saw what it was like, how peaceful it was. But then she was killed in the automobile accident." He fell silent, and Serena could empathize. For a few moments they rode in silence, until he pulled into Serena's driveway and turned off the engine.

"But that was five years ago," Carson continued. "This is now, and we're here. I wouldn't be anywhere else on earth at this very moment in time." He reached out, took her hand, and drew it to his lips.

The gentle pressure of his mouth sent a cascade of sensations through her, and she closed her eyes tightly for a second before pulling her hand away. "I've got to go in."

Carson got out of the car and came around to her side. He opened her door and took her arm, holding her eyes with his. "I think it's already too late to turn back," he murmured as she got out of the car.

She allowed him to lead her up the steps to the front door, and he turned to face her, gently placing a hand on each of her shoulders. The streetlights that reflected against his face washed out the natural tan to leave him looking pale. "You know, you don't have to come with me to the lake Saturday if you don't want to, but your family is invited. Shouldn't they have the opportunity to accept if they want?"

Serena sighed in exasperation. "You don't give up easily, do you?"

"Alternative is in good hands. I know, because I've met some of your volunteers. Have faith in them. Serena, I told you, I'm a lonely man. I need companionship, especially since I met you. I enjoy your family very much. I have a cabin cruiser with room for everyone. If not for yourself, at least let the girls have some fun."

"Okay, I give up." Serena couldn't believe what she was saying. How long had it been since she'd been out of touch with the clinic for a whole day? But Carson was right, she had good people, and she needed a break. "Sharon can take care of things for the day, and she knows others to call if she needs help. I'll ask my family."

Carson drew her to him once again and kissed her, and the touch of his lips seared hers with tingling warmth that stirred a longing within her that she never wanted to feel again.

"Good night, Serena."

❧

Edward sat at his old electric typewriter and read what he had just written. He couldn't believe his good fortune. But wasn't this the way things were supposed to work? It paid to have friends in unusual places. For instance, computer experts who could hack into the clinics in Columbia and find one Kirby Acuff, age fifteen, who'd had an abortion two years ago. The same Kirby Acuff who was now associated with Serena Van Buren at Alternative and whose parents had left the place extremely upset just the other night.

It wasn't hard to put things together, especially not for Edward, who'd had experience at it. What concerned him now was that he might have come on too strong to Serena's mother-in-law, Blythe Van Buren. He didn't want to frighten them away. He wanted them on his side. He would have to keep things cool tomorrow night at the board meeting. Besides, he didn't want his Save-a-Life group to be a laughingstock. He had a mission to fulfill.

eleven

Friday evening, Serena was tired. It had been a long, busy week, and she had been called Wednesday night to deliver a baby. It was always the most joyful part of her job, but also the most wearying. She dropped her purse on the kitchen counter and kicked off her shoes to carry them to the bedroom.

All at once, the angry sound of a loud car engine pierced the air, followed quickly by the harsh squealing of tires. Serena's brows drew together in annoyance. The front door slammed loudly enough to vibrate the windows, and someone stomped down the hall and into one of the bedrooms, slamming that door behind her, too. It had to be Jenny.

"Danny," Serena told herself with exasperation. She walked down the hall to her older daughter's room and knocked. "Jenny, I already know half the story. Do you want to tell your curious mother the rest?"

A few seconds later, a teary-eyed Jenny with windblown brown hair pulled the door open, looked at Serena, and stomped back to plop down on her bed. "What half do you know?"

"Only what the noises tell me. You and Danny had a fight."

Jenny placed her pillow onto her lap and punched it. "He asked me to go steady again."

Serena perched on the other end of her daughter's bed. "And you refused."

"Good guess," Jenny said, in a perfect imitation of her mother's dry tone. She placed the pillow behind her back. "He's threatening to go out with other girls."

"And?"

104

"And I told him to go ahead."

Serena watched the conflicting emotions in her daughter's face. "You're not crazy about the idea, are you?"

"No, but I'm tired of arguing with him. Besides, there's this cute new guy at church, and he's polite, and respectful, and you said yourself that I'm too young to go steady, and—"

Serena raised a hand to interrupt her daughter's flow of words. "You don't have to convince me."

Jenny crossed her arms behind her head. "You've always told me that love is more than physical attraction. Danny laughed at me today when I tried to tell him that there should be more of a sharing of spirits. Oh, speaking of the spiritual, there's going to be a great movie tonight; may Kirby and I use the van to go?"

"Sounds fine to me," Serena replied. "I don't think I'll need it tonight. I plan to spend a nice, quiet evening here at home."

As soon as Jenny went to take a shower, Emily Ann came banging in through the front door and stopped to stare at Serena. "Mom! Aren't you dressed yet? We've got to be there in forty-five minutes."

"Be where?"

Emily placed her hands on her hips, looking at Serena reproachfully. "Mom, you promised to be in the discussion group at the school board meeting. Don't tell me you forgot."

Serena gasped in dismay. "I already promised Jenny she could have the van to go to the movies tonight. I guess I'll have to use your granny's car."

"No, Granny's got a meeting tonight, remember?"

Serena grimaced. The Save-a-Life meeting. "Then I guess we'll have to call a taxi."

"You could buy Jenny that car she's been wanting so things like this don't happen so often."

"She's working to save money to buy that car. I wouldn't want to rob her of the thrill of doing it herself."

Emily shrugged. "Okay, Mom, but you better hurry and call that taxi. We don't have much time left, and I have to set up the refreshment stand." She turned and dashed back down the hallway to her room, then stopped and turned back. "Oh, by the way, did I tell you Carson was going to speak at the meeting, too?"

"No."

"Well, he is." She disappeared into her room.

Serena sighed. So that was the secret. Carson was going to be there. Sweet little matchmaking Emily had hopes for Carson to become a part of the family, and she was willing to manipulate everyone to see her dreams come true.

Forty-five minutes later, they stepped out of the taxi. It was a surprisingly large crowd for a school board meeting, but it wasn't hard to find Carson among the people. His tall form and dark head stood out, overpowering the rest—at least to Serena.

"See you later, Mom. Nicki's already up there," Emily said, pointing to a counter surrounded by large bottles of soda, coffee, cookies, and chips.

Serena watched her daughter skip over to the stand and crawl beneath the counter, chattering excitedly to her girlfriend as she did so, although their voices were lost in the crowd. The sight of Carson weaving his way toward Serena made her forget about her daughter's matchmaking tactics for the time being.

"Are you on the agenda for tonight?" Carson asked when he drew close.

"Yes, but I didn't realize I would be talking to a big crowd. This is just a school board meeting, isn't it?"

Carson walked with her into the large multipurpose classroom reserved for the meeting. "The topic of teenage pregnancy tends to attract attention. So does debate, and we're liable to have that tonight, with Dr. Wells in attendance." He gestured toward the slender, blond man who stood talking to

Bev Jackson beside the lectern.

Serena glanced at the man in alarm. Dr. Wells performed abortions. He also lobbied for better access to abortions in Missouri and was one of the state's most vocal proponents of partial-birth abortion. Serena despised everything he stood for, and the feeling was probably mutual. She knew that, as the reputation of Alternative spread across central Missouri, its staff, and especially its founder, would be under public scrutiny. Her behavior tonight could affect the outcome of a pregnancy later. She needed to be civil.

Carson turned and glanced at a group of people walking in together. "I didn't know Blythe was coming."

Serena swung around in surprise to find her mother-in-law talking to a serious-looking young man by her side. Blythe was supposed to be at her own meeting tonight. Had the members elected to attend this one instead? Maybe the young man Blythe mentioned was asked to talk. Could that be Edward with her?

Two young women with Blythe carried stacks of leaflets, and when they entered the classroom, they started passing them out to everyone present. They wore T-shirts with the words "Abortion = Murder" emblazoned across the front. One of the girls handed a leaflet to Carson, who shared it with Serena.

It was in the form of a letter, introducing the Save-a-Life group. It announced plans to form a picket line the following week outside a clinic in nearby Columbia, which, in the words of the writer, committed murder on Missouri citizens. The byline was Edward. Just Edward.

The words were stronger than Serena would have used, not because she disagreed with his stand, but because her mission was different. Yes, she hated abortion, but her hatred of the deed couldn't be allowed to overshadow compassion for the people she was here to help. Her counselors shared the healing message of Christ with desperate, hurting young women. Edward might be able to stir up emotion, but what good did all that anger do? It was as if he was trying to incite hatred for the people caught up in the sin, instead of for the sin, itself.

"Excuse me, Serena," Blythe said, approaching her. "Edward, here, has been after me to introduce him to you. He's—"

The brown-haired, bespectacled young man stepped forward and extended his hand. "Dr. Van Buren." His voice was smooth and well modulated—almost too controlled. "I've been an admirer of yours ever since I discovered Alternative, and even more now that I've spoken to one of your volunteers and seen you in action."

Serena was in the process of taking his hand. She froze. "Oh? When was this?"

"Different times. I'm interested in your work. I think I could help you—"

"And did you also speak with my secretary?" Serena knew she was being rude, but if this was who she thought it was. . .

Without answering, Edward held his hand out to Carson, who stood beside Serena. "You must be Dr. Tanner."

"Edward, did you speak to Mrs. Acuff outside Alternative last Monday night?" Serena asked, stepping in front of him and forcing him to look at her.

His light skin flushed easily, but he didn't seem abashed. "Yes, I just happened to catch her when she came storming out of your clinic. She accused me of working for you. Is Kirby going to keep her baby this time?"

"This time? You're a friend of Kirby's?" Serena wasn't aware Kirby had told anyone else.

"Yes, well. . .she doesn't exactly know me. I only hope she makes the right—"

"Excuse me," Carson said, "but how do you presume to know anything about Kirby's situation if she doesn't know you?"

This time the flush was darker, and Edward glanced around at the crowd uncomfortably; but before he could reply, the school board chairman spoke into the microphone and called Carson and Serena to the front.

Serena stared hard at Edward, then reluctantly turned to follow Carson to the tables set up for the forum. Who had broken Kirby's confidence, and why was Edward involving himself in her life? He was in the possession of information that had nothing to do with him.

One of the speakers ahead of Serena was Dr. Wells. He described what he did as a logical, compassionate way to rescue teenagers who were too young to handle parental responsibilities. He came across as an intelligent, caring person. Serena found herself wondering if it was possible to be that logical and not realize the presence of a human soul in the womb. She had to remind herself that her mission here was not to argue or debate, but to share with as many people as possible about Alternative. She struggled to keep her mouth shut.

Edward did not. Before Dr. Wells made his concluding remarks, Edward came marching down the center aisle with several of the Save-a-Life members. Blythe was not among them.

"I object!" Edward shouted. "You call yourself a doctor? You take lives for a living! You're a killer, a murderer!" His face was red and beaded with perspiration. He raised a fist in the air as he spoke. "You have no right to talk about compassion and responsibility. You should be behind bars! You should be executed. How would you like that, Wells, to be aborted from the earth the way you murder babies?" His voice broke, and passion and pain filled his eyes.

Bev Jackson sprang from her chair and rushed around the table to his side. She reached for him, but he suddenly swung around to face Serena and Carson. "Tell them, Dr. Van Buren! You know what I mean, Dr. Tanner! Why don't you tell them?

You're both doctors. Is there any medical evidence to prove that partial-birth abortion is ever necessary?" Tears filled his brown eyes and spilled down his cheeks.

"No, Edward, there isn't," Serena said softly.

"It isn't taking a life to save a life, then, is it? Abortion is a convenience in this country!" He raised a fist in the air. "And let the killers pay for their convenience!"

Bev grasped his arm and whispered something to him. He lowered his fist and shook his head as tears dripped down his face. His shoulders heaved, and she embraced him and walked with him out of the room. The members of his group stood looking at the crowd in bewilderment for a few short minutes, then followed him silently.

After a moment to regroup, the discussion continued. When it came time for Serena to speak, she described Alternative and the comprehensive help they offered for pregnant women—from room and board with volunteer families in the surrounding counties, to help with education, adoption services, and medical care. Carson followed up with his insight into the lives of the teenagers he'd worked with over the years in his position as a church youth leader.

The discussion ended peacefully, and several of the parents, teachers, and board members lingered to talk to Serena and Carson afterward. Serena was handing out her second stack of Alternative pamphlets when Edward entered the classroom once more. He saw her and came toward her, and the after-meeting chatter diminished around them. His eyes were red-rimmed and his face was splotched from tears, and once again Serena felt a swell of sympathy.

"How did it feel to sit calmly by while that murderer was allowed to indoctrinate everyone in this room?" His tone held accusation, and his red eyes burned resentment.

"Excuse me, Edward?" Serena kept her voice low. "This country is founded on principles of free speech. I was given an opportunity to speak, and it was my intention to present my thoughts in a reasonable, thoughtful manner so anyone who heard Wells would also hear me and realize the truth."

"If I'd been asked to speak tonight, I would have done all I could to keep him from indoctrinating these people."

"You tried, and it didn't work, did it? I don't think a shouting match prevents anyone from having an abortion, it just makes people mad."

"It gets attention," Edward said, "which keeps the issue in the minds of the people, where it should be."

Serena held his gaze for a moment. "Edward, you're obviously passionate about your convictions, and that's admirable. I'm passionate about mine, as well. I think we'll just have to agree that we go about things differently." She held out her hand.

His thoughts were obviously active behind those intelligent, slightly disturbing gray eyes. He took her hand at last. "I guess this means you won't be at our protest in Columbia next week."

She smiled. "I'll be waiting at my clinic for all those converts you send my way."

Edward didn't return the smile. He pivoted abruptly and stalked over to Bev Jackson. Serena watched the young man in confusion for a moment, then realized someone else had stepped up beside her. She turned and found herself face-to-face with Dr. Wells.

"Dr. Van Buren," the man said, extending his hand. "You handled yourself well tonight. I was afraid the meeting was going to turn into a free-for-all for a few minutes there." He shook Carson's hand, as well. "Your description of Alternative intrigues me," he said, still speaking to Serena. "I wonder if I might visit sometime and see your facilities."

"Of course," Serena said, puzzled. "Is there a particular reason why you're interested?"

His mouth tightened in irritation. "Surely you're not as narrow-minded as your young friend over there. I thought I might inspect your clinic, then possibly refer patients to you. Not all women should have terminations, you know."

"None of them should." Serena gave him her card. "Visit us any time. I'll tell my staff to expect you."

☙

Carson could tell Serena was disturbed as he drove her home, and he was glad Emily had opted to ride home with Blythe. He needed time alone to talk to Serena, though they rode more than half the way in silence, since she was seemingly deep in thought.

"Am I a fence straddler?" she asked, not turning from her perusal of the lights of the passing city.

"You're kidding, of course."

She glanced across at him. "Edward was right tonight. I didn't protest when Wells described abortion as a perfectly acceptable birth control option."

"Neither did I. There is a time and a place for protest, Serena, and Alternative is your protest. How much stronger can your voice be?"

"Some of the things Edward said made sense."

Carson pulled into the Van Buren driveway, noting Blythe's car was still absent. He switched off the engine. "Edward is a young man in pain. Surely that was as obvious to you tonight as it was to me. He's passionate and idealistic, and I sympathize with him, but there's something else going on with him. Right now, however, I'm more concerned with you." He turned to face Serena, and he saw her startled gaze skitter away from his. "Something else is bothering you, or that little debate with Edward wouldn't make you doubt yourself like this."

She shrugged, clasping her hands together in her lap. "Maybe I'm a hypocrite. I look at things a little differently because. . ." She looked at him briefly, then took a deep breath. "Carson, you remember I told you that I didn't feel we knew each other well enough yet?"

"And do you remember what I told you? There's nothing I can learn about you that will change my mind."

"Yes, but—"

Lights flashed against the garage door, and Carson glanced around to find Blythe and Emily pulling up beside them.

"So much for confession time," Serena said dryly.

He laid a hand on her arm and squeezed. "Just remember what I said. Nothing can change my heart."

❧

On his way home, Carson couldn't stop thinking about Serena. He was still disturbed as he stepped into his dark apartment and saw the red light flashing on his answering machine. Still picturing Serena's soft, intent eyes and firm, determined chin, and her exquisite instinct to help the lost and hurting, he pressed the play button.

Carol Acuff's shaking voice rose from the speaker. "Carson, I. . .I've got to talk to you." There was a sniff. "I've got to know. . .about my daughter." She identified herself, then the machine beeped and kicked off.

Carson looked at the lighted dials of his desk clock, then picked up the phone and punched the Acuffs' number. Hal answered on the third ring. "Hello, Hal, this is Carson Tanner. Is Carol there? She left a message for me to call."

"Oh, Carson, what a mess." Hal's soft-spoken voice cracked with obvious strain. "She's gone out walking, and I'm worried about her. It's getting worse. She's picked up the phone to call Kirby at least ten times tonight, but she can't bring herself to do it. Last night she was muttering in her sleep about grandbabies." He paused for breath, and there was a shudder in his sigh. "She wants to see her grandbaby. I said something to her about it this morning, and she sat down on the side of the bathtub and cried for fifteen minutes. I think the guilt's about to kill her. I know this whole thing is about to do me in."

"Guilt?"

"Tonight. . .tonight she asked me if I thought we'd really ended a baby's life—Kirby's baby. What do I tell her?"

In spite of the pain Carson heard in Hal's voice, he felt a rush of hope. "Hal, your family needs to come to terms with the past. Talk to her about it, and let her talk to you. Opening the lines of communication is your first step, and it sounds as if that is happening. I know it's painful, but a lot of times there is healing in the pain. Your next step is to call Kirby. She desperately needs to know you care about her."

"I tried to call from work, but nobody answered. I didn't leave a message."

"Next time, leave one. She needs it."

There was a short hesitation. "I know I should have already. I just. . .it's sometimes so hard to know what's best, you know."

"Yes, I know. Now is the time to seek the truth. I'll be here for you as you and your family come to terms with it."

twelve

Saturday morning, Serena awakened with the feeling of hovering darkness. A soft breeze pushed through her opened bedroom window, billowing out the lacy curtains. She slid out of bed and stepped over to the chair by the window to watch the dawn.

Ever since she was a little girl, this had been one of her favorite things to do, watching a new day promise a new start. She found no joy in it now. She felt as if she were seeking something in its beauty, and that something continued to elude her.

The pale colors in the sky deepened slowly, until its rose and bronze beauty penetrated Serena's unhappy thoughts. Some hidden mockingbird sang out, joined by a meadowlark, and then another, until the whole tree-filled yard echoed with songs. The muted ringing of a telephone marred the music for a moment, but someone answered it.

Serena stretched and yawned, consciously pushing her depression to the back of her mind. Her family deserved to see her happy today.

A timid knock sounded at her door, and Emily stuck her head in, her brown eyes wide and—for Emily—contrite. "Mom, are you mad at me?"

"For what?"

"Matchmaking."

"So you do admit that was what you were doing last night."

"Yes. Granny didn't think it was a bad idea."

"Don't blame it on your granny. I'll forgive you on one condition—I need a rubdown. Do you want to do it now or after I shower?"

Emily's eyes danced. "I'll do it now. Lie down on the floor."

Serena obliged, lying face down and burying her chin into the amethyst Berber carpeting. Immediately, her daughter's gentle hands moved over her back in an easy, circular motion, and she could feel herself melting farther and farther down into the floor. Tense muscles from a night of restless sleep began to relax.

Rubdowns were an old family tradition. When the girls were younger they had always fought over who would get to rub down Mommy's or Daddy's back. It had been just one more expression of their love for one another.

"M-m-m, just a little more on the right shoulder. Yes, that's it. Now down a little. There." Serena's words slurred as her whole body relaxed. Gradually growing aware of the silence— something unusual with Emily—Serena frowned into the carpeting. "Emily?"

"Yes, Mom?"

"Is something bothering you?"

The massaging stopped, and Serena turned over and sat up to face her daughter. Emily leaned back against the bed and gazed thoughtfully out the window. Her almond-shaped eyes held sadness, and Serena reached across and touched the back of her hand to Emily's cheek.

"Do you realize this will be the first time we've gone to the lake together since Daddy died?" Emily asked.

So that was it. Leave it to this sentimental child to remember something like that. Of course, Jenny had also mentioned it the other day. "Yes, Sweetheart. That worried me a little. It might bring back a lot of memories."

Emily shook her head and looked up at her mother. "But don't you see? It could be a new beginning for us all, with Carson there."

A new beginning? Was that possible, with so many things from the old ending left undone, unsaid, unexplained? There were too many things about Serena's past that Jennings had never known about. Why had she kept secrets from her own husband?

Serena brushed long strands of brown hair back from Emily's face. "You like Carson a lot, don't you?"

Emily's eyes narrowed as she considered the question seriously. "Yes, I do. After Daddy died, I was sure I wouldn't ever want to see you with another man. You belonged to Daddy, and another man would make me feel like we were losing you to someone else."

"And that isn't the way you would feel with Carson?"

"No. He makes us feel included in everything. I can tell he cares for us. He's different from other men, isn't he, Mom?"

"Yes, he's different. He's very special." She reached down and wrapped a strand of her daughter's hair around her finger and twirled it absently. "But even though he's special, that doesn't mean he's necessarily going to spend the rest of his life with us." She released Emily's hair and sat back.

Emily turned confused eyes up to her mother. "Why not?"

"Because sometimes a woman can't do exactly what she wants to do. There are other people we have to consider besides ourselves."

"Like who? If Carson loves us and we love him, why can't we all be together?"

"Honey, love is a wonderful thing, but it doesn't always automatically mean marriage. I care a great deal about Carson, but marriage. . .isn't meant for everyone. I think he'll find, once he gets to know me really well, that I'm not right for him."

"Of course you are!" Emily protested indignantly. "You'd be right for any man!"

Exactly an hour later, the deep chimes of the doorbell echoed through the house, and Serena heard her younger daughter race out of her room and dash down the hall. "That's

Carson!" Emily cried. "I'll get it!"

Serena, dressed in a hot pink short set, wearing her swimsuit underneath, followed at a more leisurely pace. In spite of Carson's instructions not to take food, she had decided to pack an ice chest with soda pop and fruit. She called a greeting to Carson from the hallway and proceeded into the kitchen, but she wasn't the first one there.

Kirby, her bright blond, uncombed hair shining in the sunlight that came through the window, was leaning against the counter with a glass of milk in her hand, staring out at the sky.

She glanced around at Serena and smiled. "Ready for the lake?"

Serena nodded, looking pointedly at Kirby's housecoat. "And you're not. Why?"

Kirby shrugged, avoiding Serena's eyes. "Call me chicken."

"You're not going? Why not?"

"Oh, you know, the usual thing," Kirby replied, her voice quivering. "I–I have some morning sickness, and I might get sick on the boat."

Serena stepped closer and studied Kirby's expression. "What else? There's another reason."

Kirby's face flushed a delicate pink. She took a deep breath and turned to look back out the kitchen window. "Mother called this morning." Her eyes filled with tears, and she set her milk glass down with a shaking hand. "I guess I'm feeling homesick again." She looked at Serena. "I'm messing up so many lives. I've been so selfish."

"You didn't do this all by yourself, Kirby Acuff. You can't blame yourself for the problems of the whole world. You aren't the source of all your mother's confusion right now." Serena leaned against the counter beside Kirby. "What did she say on the phone?"

"Not much. She just asked me how I was, if I'd been getting sick, if I was eating right."

"Does that tell you anything?"

"It tells me she still doesn't want to hear about how I'm feeling inside, where it counts."

"Maybe she's just afraid to ask. I imagine she's feeling guilty, herself."

Kirby uttered a short, bitter laugh. "That'll be the day. For two years she's blamed everything on me. Why should she stop now, when I'm not even there to defend myself?"

"Maybe your absence has forced her to find someone else to blame. She's having to take a look at her own actions."

Kirby bowed her head as tears trickled down her cheeks, and Serena stepped forward and wrapped her arms around the girl. "Your parents do love you, Kirby, no matter what you believe. If they didn't, they wouldn't have been so upset." She released Kirby and stepped back, then reached up to tip the girl's chin until their eyes met. "These next few weeks are going to take some understanding on your part. You have to realize that they're weak, fallible human beings, just like the rest of us. They do and say things that hurt you, without taking into consideration the pain they may be causing you, because of their own pain. I imagine they're asking themselves why—and where—they went wrong. They're blaming themselves for your mistakes, but that's because they love you so much." Serena held Kirby's blue eyes with her own. "If your parents asked you to go back and live with them, would you go?"

Kirby looked down. "Not unless I could have my baby."

There was a quiet cough at the doorway, and they looked over to see Blythe standing there, dressed for the visit with Janet, her friend, in a cool linen shift and sandals. Her expression, however, did not reflect her excitement about the upcoming plans. Her eyes were somber, her lined face serious.

Serena stepped toward her with concern. "Blythe? Is something wrong?"

The older woman nodded her head sadly. "Kirby, I found

something in your room I don't think you meant for me to find."

Serena felt Kirby stiffen beside her. "Wh–what's that?"

Blythe held out her hand. In the palm rested a little stack of tiny, oblong white pills.

Kirby caught her breath.

"I was doing some laundry, and shook these out of the pocket of your jeans," Blythe explained. "These spilled out. What are they?"

There was a long silence. "It's. . .Mother's sleeping pills," Kirby said softly.

Blythe froze for a moment, then slowly lowered her hand to her side. "But I thought—"

"I had them in my pocket the night Serena found me on the trail." Kirby turned and raised a hand toward Serena beseechingly. "I'm sorry I lied. I said I tossed them, and I didn't. But I wouldn't have taken them, honestly." She hesitated. "At least, I don't think I would have. It's just that things were so hard at home, and I knew I could be pregnant again, and I didn't think I could go through it all over. Please don't turn me in."

Serena held her hand out to her mother-in-law, and Blythe gave her the pills. "Do you have any more of them, Kirby?"

Kirby shook her head adamantly as she held Serena's gaze. "No."

Serena stared at the tiny pills and felt a wave of defeat. "And you've had them all this time."

"I wouldn't use them now, Serena." Kirby's voice held a note of urgency in it. "I wouldn't have to. Now I know someone cares."

Serena shook her head. How could she have missed something like this? Kirby could have decided, in a moment of despair, to take an overdose, and she'd admittedly lied to her parents for years. It wouldn't be safe to leave her alone.

"You're right," she told the girl at last. "A lot of people

care. Now go and get your clothes on. You're going with us."

"But I just—"

"I'm sorry, but right now you don't have a choice." Serena used her firm voice. "If you don't go, I will stay here with you, but I'm not leaving you alone today."

Kirby closed her eyes and bent her head. "You don't believe me."

Serena placed her hand over Kirby's. "Let's just say I'm not willing to bet your life on your honesty right now."

"I'll stay here with her if she doesn't feel like going," Blythe volunteered. "I can see Janet another time, and I have some work in the garden—"

"No," Kirby said. "I'm sorry, Serena. I'll go with you. I guess I just thought. . .I don't know. . .Mother might call again. Or I might call her. And I didn't want to get in the way—"

"Enough of that, young lady," Blythe insisted. "Get to your room and get dressed. I want to see a smile on your face when you come back out of there. You're going to have a good time today. You got that?"

A flush of embarrassed pleasure stole across Kirby's face, she grinned and ducked her head as she turned to leave the kitchen.

Serena slumped against the counter. "I can't believe I missed—"

"She didn't take them," Blythe said. "You caught her in time. And I really don't think she'll do it now. Do you?"

"No, but we believed her before, too."

"And she didn't use the pills, did she? We'll just keep an eye on her and keep the communication lines open." Blythe glanced toward the door and lowered her voice. "Serena, I just got a call from Aunt Myrtle, up in Nebraska."

Serena struggled to keep up with the switch in conversation, while Blythe announced that she was going to visit Myrtle and would be gone a couple of weeks. Serena opened the lid to the ice chest and checked the contents. "I'm not sure we can stand to be without you that long."

"Yup, I'm pretty indispensable, I know," Blythe replied with a teasing glint in her eye. "And the garden will probably go to pot, and Rascal will howl all night long, like he did the first week he was here."

"What about your Save-a-Life group? You'll miss the picketing next week."

Blythe shook her head. "There could be trouble there. You saw how argumentative Edward is, and the others follow his lead."

"He's young, immature, and inexperienced."

"He's trying to get attention any way he can," Blythe said. "I can almost understand him, though. You see, he got his girlfriend pregnant three years ago. He wanted to marry her and have the baby, but she didn't want to get married. She had an abortion. Really tore him up."

"Is that when he started this group?"

"No, it was already formed, but he joined it and gradually took over. You have to hand it to him, he has a way with people. He quadrupled membership within a year. He really believes in what he's doing."

Serena frowned. "I don't know. Something about him scares me. I think you were right about the mob mentality thing. It can be dangerous."

"Looks to me like he'll have to learn the hard way, Serena, and don't go suggesting I stay to keep an eye on him. He didn't listen to you the other night, and he won't listen to me. I'll be leaving Monday."

"Hadn't you better make sure you can get a ticket before you decide?"

"Ticket? For what?"

Serena frowned and looked hard at Blythe. "For the airplane, or the bus, or whatever transportation you plan to take."

"Don't need a ticket for my own car, do I?"

Serena frowned at her. "You mean you plan to drive all the way there by yourself?"

"Nonsense. I'm only going to Lincoln. That's less than a day's drive from here. The day I can't make that drive on my own is the day I've lost my usefulness. I'll start packing when I get home tonight."

Reluctantly, Serena murmured agreement. She knew from experience that it would do no good to argue. Once Blythe set her mind on something, she wouldn't be talked out of it. Still, it would have been nice to have Blythe continue her personal investigation of the Save-a-Life group. Something about that still made Serena very uncomfortable.

thirteen

The drive to the lake with the girls on board was every bit as beautiful as it had been last week alone with Carson. The morning sunshine and fresh air gave an atmosphere of newness to the rolling hills and trees of the countryside. The day was still early, and there was very little traffic on the highway—only an occasional farmer driving into town.

The aura of quiet peacefulness was only evident outside the confines of the Saturn, however. The interior seemed to be stretched to bursting with talk, laughter, excitement. Before she climbed into the backseat, Emily Ann glanced up at Carson, flashed a dimpled smile, and asked him about the skiing arrangements. His gaze was tender as it rested on her, and Serena allowed herself a few moments of unobserved enjoyment. Carson was a handsome man, with powerfully molded face, strong brow, and shoulders of a body builder—though he seldom indulged in weight lifting. He was not afraid of thoughtful silence, but neither was he afraid of sharing his heart in intimate conversation. Serena couldn't imagine how he had remained unmarried for five years after his wife's death.

Serena sighed. To her chagrin, Carson caught the slight sound, and his eyes raised to meet hers. He winked and grinned, then flipped on the signal, slowed the car, and turned right onto a narrower road that soon curved through dense forest.

"Oh, look, Mom. We're going to Horseshoe Bend," Emily exclaimed. "Are we going to Paula's?"

"No way!" Jenny called from the backseat. "We're not, are we, Mom?"

Serena cast her daughter a reassuring glance over the seat. "No, we're not going to Paula's." Poor Jenny hadn't completely recovered from her breakup with Danny, Paula's son. "Carson's boat is down here." She turned to Carson to explain. "Our friends have a cabin down here. When we used to come down, Paula always insisted we launch our boat into the cove beside her cabin."

They passed the golf course, and Serena fell silent, her mind awash with memories. She and Jennings had golfed many rounds on that course. It was beautifully kept, as it had always been, and at this time of morning it was nearly deserted except for the occasional avid sportsman.

There must have been a heavy dew last night, because Serena could see sparkling drops of water nestling in the short cropped green grass, and a mist floated in the recesses of the trees in the valley.

The forest of oak, elm, and hickory closed in around them once more, with an occasional narrow dirt road or grass path winding back through the trees. Carson slowed the car to take the curves and roughening road at a safer pace, and Serena opened her window to allow the fragrance of morning to enter the car.

&

As the conversation continued around Carson, he couldn't prevent himself from looking at Serena. She'd been reserved with him this morning, though when he looked into her eyes he saw a special spark of attraction there. Of course she had reservations. She was a sensible woman, determined to look at all sides of a relationship before committing herself. In his heart and in his mind, he had already done that. Now he needed to find the patience to wait for her to arrive at the same decision.

That old, familiar, mossy smell of the lake drifted in through the open window along with the sounds of boat motors and splashing water. When Carson pulled to a stop near the dock, he caught a glimpse of Serena's face and saw a wealth of expressions there. There was a wistfulness in her eyes, but the corners turned up in a slight smile, as if remembering the happy times she had spent here with her family.

"Did you come here a lot?" he asked Serena.

"Oh, yes. Sometimes we came to this very landing and put the pontoon in for skiing or exploring. The exploring was always my favorite part; this lake is so interesting."

"I know. I like to do that, myself," Carson replied. "The creeks and sheltered coves abound in this area, and I've spent a lot of long hours quietly drifting in and out of them."

"Hey, remember the day our battery went dead on us, and we had to paddle back to shore?" Emily asked.

"Yeah, and we only had one paddle," Jenny added. "Dad and Mom finally just jumped in the water and towed us to shore with the rope."

"I remember!" Serena exclaimed. "My shoulders were sore for days after that."

"And how about the time Dad decided to go ashore for a picnic and got the boat stuck in the mud," Jenny remarked. "We all had to get out and push."

"That was awful!" Emily remembered. "I kept feeling things tickling my toes under the mud, and I still think it was snakes."

"I don't think snakes go under the mud, do they?" Jenny asked.

"Well, let's not just sit here reminiscing, let's get out there!" Serena exclaimed.

Carson couldn't repress a faint surge of envy. Jennings Van Buren had enjoyed a wonderful, loving family and had spent those years with the most wonderful woman in the world. He still lived on in the memories of his family, but he wasn't here to enjoy it. Carson vowed silently that, if given the chance, he would shower this family with as much love and support as Jennings had done.

He glanced at Serena and saw the wistfulness in her eyes. And the sadness. There seemed to be more in her expression than the grief of losing a husband. There was almost. . .guilt. He'd seen it before, but lately, it had been even more often in evidence. He wished she felt she could talk with him about it.

≈

The long morning shadows disappeared unnoticed amidst the noisy, often hilarious excitement on the boat in the middle of the lake. Time passed quickly and easily for Serena as she watched her daughters graduate from the tube to skis, and it wasn't until both girls had skied together along a lengthy swathe of lake that the blaring sun caught their attention.

They stopped for lunch at the unique floating restaurant, rested for thirty minutes, and hit the lake again. Serena only found a few moments to worry about how things were going at the clinic, and she resisted the urge to use her cell phone for a quick call.

Carson allowed Jenny to take the wheel for a few moments while he disappeared below deck, and when he emerged a little while later, he had changed into a pair of swim trunks. "Is anyone ready for a swim?" He took the wheel back from Jenny. "There's a good place just up in this next cove. There are even some good rocks for diving, if you feel like it."

As he turned the boat into the cove, everyone except Serena followed his example and rushed below deck. Serena remained seated beside him, all her concentration directed to keeping her eyes away from the rippling muscles of his powerful shoulders and legs.

He glanced across at her questioningly. "You're quiet today, Serena. Is something wrong?"

"Nothing at all. In fact, this is all too good to be true—you're too good to be true—and we can't continue to take advantage of you. You've spent this whole day pulling skiers, feeding us, and showing us the best places to swim. I haven't seen you ski, and judging by the assortment of equipment you have on board, you must enjoy the sport more than most."

Carson slowed and stopped the boat, then turned to look at her more closely. Once more, she thought she detected a hesitance in his manner, a question in his eyes. Then without a word, almost as if he couldn't stop himself, he reached across, drew her to him, and kissed her tenderly.

He released her. "If it makes you feel better, I'll ski after we swim."

"That's better," Serena said, struggling to maintain her equilibrium after his gentle assault on her senses.

"I'll tell you what," he said as he dropped anchor, "since you're feeling so guilty, I'll let you drive the boat for me."

"You trust me?" Serena teased.

"Yes, I trust you," Carson assured her, suddenly serious. "You are trustworthy."

She shook her head. He was wrong. So wrong. "Carson Tanner, you're far too special for my peace of mind," she whispered.

"Good. Keep thinking those nice things about me," he teased.

She looked away. Every moment she spent with him made things more confusing. She had fallen in love with him. . .and he thought she was trustworthy.

❧

Edward and eight other members of Save-a-Life finished folding the last batch of fliers and stacked them in boxes to divide among the other members of their group and broadcast them across the city tonight. He was especially proud of this issue, though he was aware there might be some difficult consequences. That was okay, though. What he was doing was worth suffering for.

Sixteen-year-old Pam, the group's youngest member, gave

him her stack. "Are you sure this is legal, Edward? Did the girl give you permission to print this? She might not want everyone to know her past."

"I didn't name names, did I?"

"No, but names were all you didn't put in here."

"Look at it this way, Pam, the story needs to be told. Besides, before long everyone will know she's pregnant."

"Sure, then those who know about it will also know everything else."

"Believe me, she won't be the only pregnant senior in high school."

Pam shook her head. "But what about Dr. Van Buren and Alternative? You're really raising questions in everybody's minds, and what if she's bona fide? You could ruin her whole program and hurt the cause. You did name names there."

Edward smiled and tugged a strand of the girl's hair. "If anything goes wrong, you can tell everybody you told me so, okay?"

Pam shook her head, turned away, and left with two of the other girls.

Edward's smile died as the others filed out of the room ahead of him. Sure, Pam was only sixteen. A kid. Badly as he hated to admit it, she had a point. It was too late to back out now, after he already had the fliers printed and the group prepared to pass them out. But Pam had a lot of common sense. She had worked on the school newspaper her sophomore year, and she had a good reputation for reporting the truth. Of course, it was just a school paper—but wasn't that all Edward, himself, had ever worked on? Maybe he should watch Alternative a little more before he made his final decision. Maybe he still didn't know all there was to know about Serena Van Buren. Maybe he would dig a little deeper, find out what kind of connection she had with that abortionist, Dr. Wells.

fourteen

On Monday, Carson managed to convince Carol and Hal Acuff to meet them for a trial family conference that evening at Alternative. As Serena drove downtown with Kirby, she could feel the tension radiating from the pretty teenager.

"Mother'll lose her temper like she always does," Kirby predicted.

"Possibly not. Perhaps she'll curb it tonight."

"Whether she does or not, I'm going to say what I think, Serena." Kirby crossed her arms over her chest.

Serena patted Kirby's shoulder encouragingly. Things would work out with this family. Carol Acuff wanted her daughter back, and she was a determined lady. If she had to show more unselfish love toward her family, Serena didn't doubt that Carol would eventually break old habits and find a way to reach out.

The familiar landmark of the capitol building appeared too soon for Serena; she wasn't looking forward to this meeting. She wished she wasn't so emotionally involved.

They both remained in a thoughtful mood until they parked close to the clinic, then Kirby glanced across at Serena, her blue eyes wide and apprehensive. "You sure they want me back?"

"Positive. Tonight's meeting will just be to pinpoint some problem areas."

To Serena's relief, the air-conditioning in the clinic had been left on, and she felt its invigorating coolness as she led the way back to the little conference area they had used exactly a week earlier. As before, the others weren't there yet, and the two of

130

them sat down side-by-side on the sofa.

Kirby held out trembling hands and expelled a deep sigh. "Can you tell I'm nervous?"

"Your parents will be nervous, too. Your mother has had a chance this past week to think about some things. She may be having trouble dealing with them, just as you are."

"I know you keep saying that, but it's hard to imagine my mother admitting she's wrong." Kirby leaned her head against the high back of the sofa. "When I was a little girl, I believed she could do no wrong. She was strong, she knew what she wanted, and Dad and I always went along with her because it made life easier. I never resented it until I started high school. That was when she started getting on my nerves. She told me what classes to take, what clubs to join, and she was never satisfied with less than A's on my report cards. After awhile, I realized I didn't know how to satisfy her anymore, so I quit trying. I think my father realized a long time ago there was no pleasing her, so he just kind of went into his quiet little shell."

"That can change," Serena said. "You and your mother will have to learn to talk to each other. She needs to understand that you aren't a child any longer."

Kirby nodded. "Jenny's been talking to me a lot this week about God and about how He made us the way we are, with our own thoughts and feelings." Her voice tapered off as she stared thoughtfully out the window, then she asked, "Do you think if I told God I was sorry about the abortion and everything, He could forgive me?"

"Of course."

"And take all that away?"

"All what?"

"All the sin?"

"Yes. It will never be like it was before, and here on this earth you will always face the results of the choices you made, but you will have an eternity with God. You won't pay for those sins after you die." As she spoke, the front door opened, and she could feel Kirby tense.

"Brace yourself," the girl said softly as Carson preceded Hal and Carol Acuff into the conference room.

Carson gave them a smile and walked toward them. Serena could tell he was nervous by the tense set of his shoulders. "Hi," he said. "Hot enough for you outside?"

"Hi, Carson." Kirby dipped her head and studied her hands, clasped tightly in her lap.

Carol Acuff didn't say anything, but Serena saw the woman's face soften as she looked at her daughter. Serena got up from the sofa and stepped forward. "Hal and Carol, I'm glad you're here. Do you want anything to drink? We have a soda machine, and we keep cookies in the kitchenette in back."

"No, thank you," Carol said coolly as she lowered herself onto the sofa beside her daughter, where Serena had been sitting. Her eyes darted over Kirby, then back to Serena. "Well, she looks none the worse for her week with you," she observed reluctantly. "Has she been behaving? None of that staying out till all hours of the night?"

"None at all," Serena assured the woman. "I think my girls have kept her so occupied, she didn't have time to get bored."

Kirby looked up at last. "We swim a lot in their pool, and Jenny and I went to a movie Friday night, but we got back early." She leaned forward. "Saturday we all went to the lake with Carson."

Carol cast a less than friendly look at Serena. "No wonder Kirby wanted to stay with you. Swimming parties, trips to the lake—"

"No one bribed me to stay with them, Mother," Kirby said with a scowl. "But I did feel wanted there, and they didn't try to force me to do anything I didn't want to do or set impossible standards for me that I couldn't meet."

"Impossible standards? You mean like not getting pregnant? Apparently that's too much to—"

"Stop it!" Kirby stood to her feet. "I thought we were going to try to communicate. How many times did I tell you I was sorry? You don't listen! You never listen! What good does it do to try when I can never please you?" She paced across the room, arms crossed protectively over her chest.

Carol's eyes flashed fire. "As if you—"

"That's enough. Stop right there." Carson's calm voice was suddenly filled with steel as his gaze flicked from Carol to Kirby. "We came here to talk, and that isn't what we're doing. Hal and Carol, I feel I need to stress the value of having a professional counselor meet with your family for the—"

"No." Carol raised a hand to her face and rubbed her forehead wearily. "It didn't work last time, it won't work now." She shook her head and sighed.

Hal cleared his throat nervously. "Maybe if we tried again. Maybe if we tried harder this time. Obviously, what we're doing isn't working. We've got to change."

Carol blinked at him, lips parting in surprise.

"You never listened to Kirby," Hal continued. He cleared his throat again and sat forward, hands clasped together between his knees. "You never listened to me, either. Kirby never had a chance to make her own decisions. How could she learn—"

"How dare you talk to me like that!" Carol snapped. "Who was supposed to make the decisions for the family if I didn't? My houseplants have more backbone than you do! When's the last time you gave me any help with Kirby? When's the last time you ever punished her?"

Hal's face reddened. "Why should I punish her? You were always too glad to do it."

Carol gasped. "And you would have let her run out and play in the street, for all you cared about discipline. When I married you, I thought I was marrying a real man. Imagine my shock when—"

"Maybe you didn't let me be a real man," Hal retorted, his face splotching with color. "Maybe you didn't give me a chance. I could've handled the money. Just because you didn't agree with the way I handled it, you took over. And Kirby was a good baby, but you wanted perfection." He had lost all his nervousness now and was leaning forward in his seat, pinning his wife with his gaze. "Just because I didn't punish her doesn't mean I didn't help you with her. Many's the time I got up in the middle of the night to feed her, and many's the diaper I've changed."

"Changing diapers isn't all there is to raising a kid," Carol snapped.

Kirby laughed suddenly, a short, bitter laugh. "Would you listen to yourselves? I'm not a baby in diapers anymore. In a few months, I'm going to have a baby of my own. Mother, I have feelings and opinions, and I actually do have a brain, believe it or not. Can't you see that? If you can't, I may never be able to go back home with you."

Carol's face grew pale. "How can you say that to me?"

"Oh, stop the dramatics, Mother," Kirby snapped. "You've played that guilt game too many times. Why don't you concentrate on perfecting yourself before you fix the rest of the world?"

Carson raised a hand for silence. "Time for a cool-down."

"But she's—"

"No, Carol," Carson said firmly. "Stop and think about what you're saying. It's useless to place blame now. What the three of you need to realize is that you've all made mistakes. All of us do. Instead of pointing fingers, it's time to concentrate on learning from those mistakes in order to improve your family relationship. Carol and Hal, you can't continue blaming your daughter for a decision she made and now regrets. She needs your support, and you can give that only if you can escape the blame game."

"I agree with Carson," Serena said. "And if we may, we would like to continue working with you and Kirby on a weekly basis, no matter where Kirby lives. Just knowing you want her back has helped her, but it doesn't clear up a lot of the deep problems you still have as a family. She still needs guidance."

Carol stood and paced across the room, shaking her head in obvious frustration. She stopped to study a picture on the wall of a mother staring with delight into the face of her newborn baby. For a long moment, the others waited in uncomfortable silence. When she turned back there were tears in her eyes. "You don't think this family is beyond help?"

"No, you aren't," Carson said. "You can have profitable family conferences, you can learn to communicate instead of shouting. Serena has a very caring, reputable family counselor on staff. We could schedule sessions in the evenings," he raised an eyebrow at Serena, who nodded, "so neither of you will have to take off work."

"We've got to do something," Hal said. "Carol?"

Carol shot her husband a resentful look, then bent her head. "What choice do we have, if we want to get Kirby back?"

Serena stifled a sigh of relief, then glanced at Kirby. "You have a vote, too. What do you want to do about this?"

Kirby looked at her mother's bowed head uncertainly. "I want to try it. Maybe it'll work, if we all try to get along."

"Carol," Serena said, "if you spend some time on the phone with Kirby this week—maybe for just a few minutes every day—I think you'll realize how much talking does help. Try to listen to her as if she were a friend, an equal. I'm not saying you can't be a mother or that she won't have restrictions, but try as much as possible to treat her like an adult."

Carol leveled a cold stare at Serena, then turned to her

husband. "Well, Hal, is it okay with you if we go home now?" Her voice was heavy with sarcasm. "We can set up another meeting next week."

&

"Ouch! Rascal, stop biting my foot!" Emily jerked her spoon sideways at the dinner table and scattered droplets of soup over Kirby's plate.

Jenny poked Kirby with her elbow and giggled at a joke Kirby had just told. Serena sat back in her chair and sighed. At least there was a semblance of normal family life here for the lonely teenager to draw from. The peace was welcome. Now if only she could avoid getting any calls from the hospital tonight, she might be able to relax and rest, but before she finished her meal the telephone rang. She sighed, laid down her napkin, and went into the kitchen to answer it.

"What have you done?" The voice was soft, strangely hoarse, intense. It certainly wasn't the hospital or a nervous patient. This woman sounded as if she were in shock. It was Carol Acuff. For a moment, Serena wondered if the woman had lost touch with reality. "I'm sorry, I don't understand what you mean."

"Why did you. . .how could you tell them?"

"Carol, what's wrong? What are you talking about?"

"I should never have listened to you! You said everything would be confidential, and now it's being spread all over the city!"

Serena glanced toward the dining room, where the others continued their conversation, unaware of the problem. "Carol," Serena said gently. "Just tell me what's happened. What's upsetting you?"

"Did you think I wouldn't be upset to find our family's life story in print, scattered all over town in those stupid fliers by that meddler?"

A cold suspicion grew in Serena's mind. "Who?"

"That fool who accosted me outside your clinic last week."

"Did you actually see a flier?"

"I'm holding it in my hand! How could this happen?"

"Was the man's name Edward?"

There was a long silence, then, "I don't. . .I'm not. . .sure."

"Listen to me, Carol, I would never do anything like that, but I might know who did. The man who talked to you the other night? The first time I met him was last Friday night at a school meeting, and I didn't share anything with him, but he tried to question me about you. He told me he had spoken with you. Please believe I would never do this. Neither would Carson."

There was a sound of broken crying. "I sure didn't tell him all this."

"Why don't you read it to me over the—"

"Not now. I can't deal with this right now. It isn't bad enough that my own daughter has left me to live with some rich. . .just leave me alone." She hung up.

Serena dialed the number back. It was busy. She hung up and dialed Carson's home number. He answered on the first ring. "Carson, it's Serena. Carol Acuff just called me, and she sounds frantic. Remember Edward from the meeting the other night?"

"How could I forget?" he asked dryly.

"He's apparently printing more fliers, and this one has Carol very upset."

"Any idea what it's about?"

"Kirby."

"What about her?"

"I don't know, but Carol feels as if he's printed their family story."

There was a low, tired groan over the line. "This is getting scary, Serena. I've been checking out some web pages online. There's an interactive site that makes me think of Edward. It starts off with a clear, pro-life theme; but as I pulled up more pages, the message grew dark, angry, filled with hatred, the way Edward behaved the other night. I researched some of the pro-life groups in central Missouri today, and three people have warned me to beware of Edward. He has some real problems."

"He could do a lot of damage."

"I think I'll drive over and visit the Acuffs tonight," Carson said. "I want to take a look at that flier. Want to go with me?"

"I'll let you handle this one. I think Carol's had all of me she can take for one day."

❧

"Are you sure these will work?" Edward asked the man in the back room of an old storage building out in the country. He darted a glance over his shoulder into the shadows. This place was scary. This man was scary.

"They'll work," snapped the shadowed bulk in front of him. "Give me the cash. And this better not be a trick!"

"Trick?" Edward tried to keep the squeak out of his voice. He cleared his throat and handed the man the new bills he'd gotten at the bank just this afternoon. He was doing the right thing. He knew he was. The people of Jefferson City would be shocked out of their selfish, complacent attitudes. They would know what Serena Van Buren did down at that clinic.

"Now, could you tell me, just one more time, how to set these?"

"I told you once, and that's enough!" the man growled. "And if anyone finds out about this, I'll come after you."

Edward swallowed. "But I didn't write any directions down. What if—"

The shadow shoved the box of explosives into Edward's chest. "You didn't pay for written directions." He swung around and walked off, and Edward didn't have the nerve to try again. He could get on the Internet. Someone there would know.

fifteen

Carson wasn't sure of his welcome when he knocked at the front door of the Acuff residence, but when Hal answered the knock he looked relieved. "Thank goodness, Carson. Come in."

Carol strode into the living room from the kitchen, hands on hips, her lips set in a grim line. Her eyes were puffy and red-rimmed from crying. "I guess Serena called you."

"Yes, she's worried about you."

"Please have a seat," Hal said. "We need to talk about this."

Carson sat down on the edge of a plush blue sofa and leaned forward, elbows on knees. "Serena told me how upset you were. May I see the flier?"

Carol hesitated, then picked up a trifolded paper and handed it to him. "I don't know where this guy got his information."

"He said he talked to you outside the clinic last week. Do you remember anything you told him?"

Carol shook her head and sat down. Her face was pale and drawn, and her blond hair tumbled across her forehead in messy disarray. "I sure didn't tell him my life story, or Kirby's. Just read it, and you'll see what I mean. Doesn't make Alternative look too great, either. The guy's crazy."

Carson read quickly, noting that the Acuff name was never mentioned, though it was Kirby's story. In a graphic, fictionalized account, it told about her past abortion, then hinted with sly innuendo that she was pregnant again. He expressed in vivid detail how upset Carol had been the night he spoke to her.

". . .she knew to look past that gentle, storefront facade, to the wicked lies within, and she came out a changed woman.

139

What will happen to her daughter now? They thought they had found help. . . ."

Carson read on, his frown deepening when he came to the barely disguised character of Serena and the question Edward left dangling for the reader to interpret.

"Clinic founder. . .friend or foe? Is this clinic really pro-life, or is that just what she wants us to believe? There are many people in our country who want a baby badly enough to pay tens of thousands of dollars on the black market, but who will pocket the money for this girl's baby? Is that what this fight is all about, or should we delve more deeply still? The sympathies of this particular OB/Gyn are in question. It has been suggested that this clinic could even be another front for the killers. Of course, that remark comes from an irate and frantic mother. Draw your own conclusions. . . ."

Carson stood up, dropped the leaflet on the coffee table, and took a deep breath to control his mounting anger.

Carol slowed her pacing steps. "I didn't think I was talking to some stupid, half-cocked reporter that night." Her voice was defensive now. "I was mad, and who could blame me? My own daughter had chosen to live with someone besides me. I didn't mean. . .I didn't think. . . ."

"I know." Carson picked up the flier, then threw it back down again.

"But we didn't know," Hal said. He stepped forward and hesitantly put an arm across his wife's shoulders. "Once Carol thought about it, she realized that you and Serena didn't know, either."

"I wonder how many fliers they printed," Carol asked.

"Just be glad he didn't use your name."

❧

It had been two hours since Serena called Carson, and when the telephone rang she grabbed up the receiver. She was surprised to hear Carol Acuff's voice at the other end of the line.

"Carol, are you okay?" Serena asked with a rush of relief.

"I. . .I guess," the woman said reluctantly, then in a rush, "I don't guess you could have told that fool anything. I wasn't thinking too straight when I called. I. . .I'm s–sorry. I want to meet with you and Kirby again, the way we planned."

Serena didn't betray her surprise. "Good. Thank you. I would like to read the flier, if you don't mind. Could you save it for me?"

There was a pause. "Well. . .it says some things you won't like. He even quoted me when I was angry last week. It may not be the best—"

"I promise not to hold it against you," Serena assured her. "But if we're battling an enemy, I would like to know how to prepare myself."

"Carson took a copy of it. I guess he'll probably show it to you."

Serena set up an appointment for the following week and hung up, elated by Carol's apology, worried about what might have been printed about the clinic. What if Edward frightened potential patients away? He was hurting the very cause he professed to support.

❧

Edward was either not at home or refused to answer Carson's persistent knock. After ten minutes trying at both front and back entrances to the man's apartment, Carson gave up—but only for tonight. Edward needed help, and Carson wanted some answers.

❧

The remainder of the week passed slowly, and Blythe's absence affected Serena the most. She hadn't realized how much she had depended on Blythe's easy companionship and common sense, on their peaceful evening ritual listening to the girls splash in the pool or talking on the phone. As Blythe had predicted, the garden suffered without her loving hand,

and Serena had no time to care for it.

Blythe would also have helped transporting teenagers across the city to youth rallies and shopping for school clothes and all those wonderful summer activities that seemed to converge on them at once. Serena found herself especially busy with a new onslaught of patients at her office. Several women visited Alternative, and Serena was relieved that the fliers Edward published were, for the most part, ignored.

Thursday, Serena received a call in her office from Jenny.

"Mom, can Kirby and I spend the weekend at Paula's cabin? She said we could use it, and she's going to be out of town."

"I don't know. . . ." Serena glanced at the clock. Her next patient was due to walk in any time. "I don't like the idea of you two young girls being down there alone. The cabin does not have a phone. What if something went wrong?"

"Mom, what could go wrong? We can take the cell phone. There's a neighborhood watch down there, and all the doors have triple locks, which you know Paula never uses because it's so safe," Jenny reminded her.

"What do you plan to do all weekend, sit around the house?"

"Of course not. Paula said we could use the boat if we were careful. We won't go skiing or anything, but I'd like to explore." Jenny paused for a moment, as if thinking up more things to do at a moment's notice. "We could always go shopping at one of those tourist traps that have overpriced junk for sale, or to the amusement park in Osage Beach. If you want, I can call you Saturday night to let you know everything's okay."

Serena glanced at her clock again. "So what made you decide all of a sudden that you had to spend this weekend down at Paula's cabin?"

"Actually, it's for Kirby. You know she said she might go home next week, and her parents may not let her go anywhere like that. She's never stayed on the lake before, and for both of

...s, it's our last big chance for a little freedom before school starts."

"Who's going to be there besides you and Kirby? Any other friends?"

"No, just me and Kirby."

"Does Danny know you'll be there?"

Jenny hesitated, and Serena held her breath. "I don't know, Mom, but I don't think Paula will tell him. She knows how I feel about him."

"And how is that?"

"Mom, I thought you could read my mind. Besides, I told you just the other day that I didn't care if he dated other girls. . .or at least, that's what I told him."

"But you also admitted it might bother you. Honey, what would you do if he showed up at the cabin and decided he was staying, too? After all, it is his family's cabin."

Jenny hesitated again, then said, "Kirby and I would leave. It's all we could do. Kirby's just now beginning to listen to me when I talk about God, and if I were to compromise myself, I'd be proving to her that I'm the kind of a hypocrite her mother keeps telling her about." She added more softly, "Even if I wanted to stay, I wouldn't."

Serena glanced up worriedly as her next patient entered her office. "Okay," she said reluctantly, lowering her voice. "I guess you can go, but we'll talk more about it when I get home tonight."

"Thanks Mom. Oh, I forgot to ask if we could use the van. . . will you be needing it this weekend?"

"Only if I want to go anywhere," Serena replied dryly.

"Oh. And do you?"

"Well, there's a sidewalk sale downtown this Saturday morning. . . ."

"Please, Mom?"

Serena's eyes flicked across the desk to her patient, who

was trying hard to look disinterested in her conversation. "Okay, I suppose I could take a taxi if I really need to go anywhere."

"Great. One more thing I forgot to tell you. Dr. Wells visited the clinic today."

"Oh, really? Did Sharon give him a tour?"

"Yes. He didn't say much about it, but he said if he gets any women in his office who might be interested, he'll send them our way. Do you think he will?"

"I hope so."

"Oh, yeah, and you know that guy who was hanging around outside the clinic the other day? He was back."

"Did he come into the clinic?"

"No." There was a pause. "But he was outside when Dr. Wells came in."

Serena nearly groaned aloud. That was all they needed. He would think they were an abortion clinic for sure now.

sixteen

Friday evening Serena sat cross-legged on the floor in the family room, folding a huge pile of donated maternity clothes while Rascal eyed her activity with concentrated interest. The puppy crouched beside the sofa until Serena had three neat stacks of blouses and jeans, then he romped across the floor with his floppy ears flying. With a growl of attack, he grabbed a pair of jeans in his sharp teeth and started to shake them.

Serena made a quick rescue before he could do any damage. "Dog! I'll send you outside if you're not careful!"

He turned and looked up into her eyes with sudden, soulful mourning.

"No more."

He scampered forward without warning and licked her face before she could stop him.

She never could resist a sloppy kiss. She leaned back against the sofa and scratched behind his ears. "Poor thing. I guess you miss Blythe, don't you?"

He licked her again and laid his head against her arm.

"Yeah, so do I."

"So do I," echoed a small, forlorn voice from the kitchen doorway, and Serena looked up to find her younger daughter slouching into the room, long brown hair tumbling across her face, mouth drooping.

"I know, Honey." Serena released the puppy. "Don't worry. Granny will be back home soon. Isn't she supposed to call tonight?"

Emily plopped down on the floor and picked up a dress to fold it. "Tomorrow night."

"Where are Jenny and Kirby?"

"Back in their rooms, packing." Emily pushed Rascal away from the dress she held. "Did you know they're going to take Rascal with them? They've already packed the dog food."

"Yep. Sorry, Sweetie, it's just you and me this weekend."

Emily folded another dress, then reached out absently and rubbed Rascal's head. She glanced up at Serena. "Hmm." Deep in those golden brown eyes, a little twinkle stirred to life.

That always made Serena nervous. "What do you mean, 'Hmm?' "

A tiny smile played around Emily's lips. She ducked her head and folded another dress.

"Emily Ann, what are you up to?"

"Oh, nothing, Mom. I just thought of something." She leaned back against the sofa and looked up at Serena. "With Granny and Jenny both gone, I won't have anyone to take me to church. I guess if you won't take me, I won't get to go."

Serena knew immediately that she was caught, but for a moment she played along. "Sorry, Honey, we don't have a car. It won't hurt you to miss one service, will it?"

Emily's eyes flew wide. "Mom!"

"Gotcha." Serena chuckled as she heard the other two girls coming down the hallway. "I can't let my younger child backslide on me, can I?"

"You mean you'll go?"

"I'll go to church with you so you won't have to go alone."

"All right! Hey, Jenny, guess what," she said as the girls came chattering and laughing into the room. "Mom's going to church with me Sunday!"

Jenny's face reflected her sister's joy, and Serena realized once more, with a pang, how difficult her nonattendance had been on her family.

"Under one condition," she warned, indicating the huge

stacks of folded and unfolded clothing around her. "That I don't get buried underneath all of this before Sunday morning."

Jenny and Kirby looked at each other, then sat down and started folding. "We can take this by the clinic on our way out of town," Jenny said.

"Good." Serena reached over and tore a slip of paper from a pad. "And here's the address of Memorial Baptist Church. They've collected four boxes of baby blankets, clothing, diapers, and a crib. I need you to pick it up on your way back into town Sunday evening and deliver it to the clinic."

"Sure, Mom."

"I packed an ice chest with food. It's on the kitchen counter. Don't forget to put it in the van."

Jenny smiled at Serena. "Steaks for barbeque?"

"And fruit and vegetables and sandwich supplies. There are a couple of board games on the counter I thought you might want to take with you since Paula doesn't have a television."

Kirby looked from Serena to Jenny and shook her head. "I'll never have that kind of a relationship with my mother."

"What do you mean?" Serena asked.

"You treat each other with. . .such respect. You can talk to each other. You do things for each other. There's so much love, and it just kind of spills out, you know?"

"Well, Kirby, we're starting to kind of like you, too," Jenny teased. "Maybe you could just hang around here with us."

"And while you're at it," Serena said, "pick out which of these clothes you want."

"You mean you're giving me maternity clothing?"

"Sure," Serena said. "You're pregnant, aren't you? Eventually, you'll need to size up."

The expression of dismay on Kirby's face made Jenny and Emily giggle. Kirby picked up a light blue dress, then discarded it. "Not my size."

"How do you know what size you'll be in a few months?" Jenny teased.

Kirby held the size tag under Jenny's nose. "I refuse to gain four sizes! If I do, I won't need this dress, because I'll hide in the house with the sheet over my head until I have the baby."

Jenny laughed, then sobered. "That would be awful. Then you couldn't even go to church with me."

Kirby picked up another dress and considered it. "Maybe your church wouldn't want me if they knew I was an unwed mother."

"Of course they'll want you," Jenny said. "Don't you remember what I told you about forgiveness the other night? If you seek God's forgiveness with a truly contrite heart, He'll forgive you; and if He forgives you, then who else has a right to accuse you?"

Kirby nodded, as if she'd been thinking about it for a while. "Serena, you believe that, too?"

"Yes." She did believe it. She'd believed it all her life, but for some reason she felt like a hypocrite saying it, because she knew, deep down, that she had been unable to apply it to herself.

Kirby picked up a pink sweater, fingered the material absently, and hugged it against her. "Serena, do you think my parents will go to church with me when I go back home?"

Serena folded a pair of maternity jeans. That was a good question. "You can ask about it during your sessions. Let them know it's important to you. Going to church is a personal decision for everyone. Your mother may not feel comfortable with it at first."

Jenny shot Serena a searching look, but said nothing.

In spite of Rascal's continued interest in their work, they soon had the clothes sorted, stacked, and boxed. Each girl carried a box to the van, then loaded her own luggage and the things Serena had packed for them. They loaded Rascal last.

The van had just pulled out of the driveway when the muted ringing of the telephone forced Serena to set her armload of diapers on the sofa. "Uh-oh, Mom," Emily said, running down the hallway toward her room, "I just remembered that Granny wanted me to keep an eye on the garden."

Serena picked up the receiver. "Hello."

"What a surprise," came Carson's deep, teasing voice. "I felt sure your secretary would answer for you at home, just like at the office, so you wouldn't have to talk to me."

"I didn't want to pay her overtime," she teased. "Besides, I wasn't avoiding you. I just had a very hectic week, as you must know, since you referred a couple of patients to me from the ER."

"In that case, I'll get down to business. I just talked with Carol Acuff on the phone. She tells me Kirby and Jenny are planning a trip to Horseshoe Bend this weekend."

"What did she say about it?"

"That she wished she could afford to take her own daughter to the lake."

Serena shook her head. "What she needs to afford is time to listen to Kirby."

"She's trying, Serena. She's still jealous of you, but she wants her daughter back. I know that will all work out given time. Actually, that isn't why I called. I thought you might like a ride to church Sunday, since you were kindhearted enough to allow your daughter to use the only mode of transportation for the weekend."

"And Emily clued you in to this fact," Serena said.

"My matchmaking angel. Need a lift?"

"Emily and I can take a taxi."

"I'm cheaper, and I sort of already told your daughter I would be seeing her at church."

Serena sank down onto the sofa and sighed. She was getting a little irritable about Carson and Emily ganging up on her time after time, in spite of their good intentions. "Maybe I'll rent a car for the weekend."

There was a short pause. "Uh-oh," he said quietly. "I've crossed over the line, haven't I?"

Yes, he had, but she couldn't help being impressed that he'd picked up on it. "I read this book recently, Carson. It's called *Boundaries*, and it's an excellent book. It explains the need to set parameters in our lives."

"I'm sorry, Serena. I'm pushing too hard. I don't mean to make you uncomfortable." His deep voice held sincere contrition. "I need to remind myself that, just because I want to spend time with you every chance I get, I have no right to force you into anything."

She felt a smile nudging at her lips in spite of herself. "Yes, well. . ."

"And just because I think you're very special, and beautiful, and—"

"Okay, I get the message." She grinned. "Thank you, Carson. I'm still taking a taxi to church Sunday."

"I understand."

"Please don't get me wrong, I do appreciate the offer, but it's going to be difficult. . .what I mean is. . .it's been a long time since I've gone to church."

"I know. I struggled with that after Judy's death. Serena, I know this sounds almost like blasphemy, but have you never forgiven God for taking Jennings away from you?"

She blinked in surprise. "Forgiven God?"

"Please don't take me wrong. I don't mean to say God actually needs your forgiveness, but that you might need to forgive. Several weeks after Judy died, I realized that I was still angry with God, and until I overcame that anger, I couldn't move forward in my life. In order to heal that breach, I decided to forgive Him. It was a simple act of letting go of the anger and reestablishing my connection with Him. It must not

A Living Soul 151

have been as sacrilegious as it seemed at the time, because He blessed me with a much deeper relationship with Him than I had ever experienced before."

"I think that's wonderful, Carson," Serena said softly. "But I don't need to forgive God."

"Oh?"

"It's. . .complicated."

"Do you want to tell me about it?"

She bit her lip and stared out the window, where she saw Emily working in the garden. "I haven't had a good relationship with God for. . .many years. Sometimes I wonder if I ever did, even though I was raised in a home that professed Christianity. Jennings and I got married when I was nineteen, and he put me through school. He was the most wonderful man. . .and he was four years older than me, already established in the family business. He became my whole life. He was a dedicated Christian and we were active in the church. I said all the right things, volunteered for committees, worked in the nursery, and sang in the choir."

"How did you find time to complete your education in the midst of all that busywork?"

"I postponed it for a couple of years. Jennings helped me a lot with the girls and housework. But when he died, everything suddenly came crashing down. I realized that, during all those years of marriage, I had allowed him to be my connection to God. I lived my faith through him. My focus was on my husband, not Jesus Christ. Sometimes I wonder if God took Jennings from me because of that, but then I realize that isn't possible. My spiritual walk isn't worth a man's life."

"Your soul was worth a Man's life, Serena," Carson said. "Your soul, not just Jenny's, or Emily's, or mine. You are as special to God as any of us, and you're even more special to Him than you are to me."

For a moment, Serena couldn't speak. How could she

explain to him that she had blown her chance many years ago? "Maybe we can talk more about it someday," she said.

"When? Every day counts, Serena. Every time you push God away, you build a thicker wall around—"

"Has anyone ever said you'd be a good preacher?"

"I'm doing it again, right?"

"Yes. Why don't we change the subject? Have you had a chance to find out more about Edward?"

There was a slight pause, and she could almost hear Carson's frustration over the phone line. "I haven't found him. He's apparently doing his best to avoid me."

"Jenny told me he was outside the clinic Wednesday. He was there when Dr. Wells visited."

"Oh, no."

"I wonder what he'll write next." Serena saw Emily wander out of the garden toward the house. "Carson, I need to go. Emily's looking pretty lonely, and I'm going to take her on a walk and cheer her up."

"Would the two of you be interested in a late dinner?"

"Thanks, but we've eaten."

"Okay." He sounded disappointed. "I'd risk stepping over your boundaries again and ask you and Emily to go to Columbia with me tomorrow to a boring, all-day conference, but—"

"Carson." She couldn't help smiling.

"Yes, well, I'll probably see you Sunday at church, then."

She shook her head. "You don't give up easily, do you?"

"No."

"Good night, Carson."

"Good night."

seventeen

"Morning, Mom!" The sound of Emily's voice early Sunday morning scattered the last of Serena's dream, and she pried her eyes open, then squinted at the bright light that attacked her through the open window shades.

"Morning."

"It's going to be a beautiful day, isn't it? I knew you wouldn't want those old blinds closed, so I opened them for you."

Serena yawned and turned to press her face into the scented softness of her satin pillowcase. "Lovely."

"Come on, I thought we might go for a swim before we get ready for church," Emily prompted. "What do you think?"

For perhaps the first time in a year, Serena shuddered at the thought of diving into that cool water and exercising her sleepy limbs. Last night, along with many other nights lately, she had tossed restlessly, tangling her blankets into a hopeless knot. She'd probably had less than four hours of quality sleep—but there was Emily, her golden brown eyes shining, and Serena didn't have the heart to turn her down.

"Okay. You go on ahead of me, and I'll meet you there in a few minutes."

Emily raised an expressive eyebrow reproachfully. "You'll go back to sleep."

Serena grunted, then shook her head and slid out from under the clinging covers. "Okay! I'm coming! I hope you're satisfied," she grumbled. As Emily stepped out into the hallway, Serena slipped her nightgown up over her head and replaced it with a Chinese blue, one-piece swimsuit.

153

Emily led the way to the pool through the house, and Serena studied her youngest daughter with sudden interest. "Have you been losing some weight? That suit doesn't seem to be fitting you so tightly these days." She indicated with surprise the modest green swimsuit her daughter wore.

Emily beamed at Serena. "It's about time you noticed. Granny put me on a diet about three weeks ago."

"Come to think of it, you look like you're getting taller, too. Let's measure you after this swim," Serena suggested. "I think my little girl is growing up."

Though she said it teasingly, she felt the quick sting of tears in her eyes. Her little girl was growing up. Her little girl. . .

As was usually the case, just a few minutes in her daughter's company was all Serena needed to feel alive and refreshed once more. After five laps around the pool, she felt energized enough to face her reentry to church without so much trepidation. She just hoped the energy would last. This was not a good time to face old memories.

"Mom, I wish we could call Carson and have him come and pick us up." Emily swam up beside Serena and grasped the side of the pool.

"Emily Ann, we discussed this yesterday." Serena climbed the metal steps and sat on the concrete. "I know you like to play matchmaker, but you're going too far." She squeezed water from the dripping strands of her short, blond hair.

Emily climbed out and sat beside her. "But I feel if I don't push, nothing's ever going to happen between you and Carson, and you're so perfect for each other."

"Don't worry," she said dryly, "Carson's doing enough pushing for both of you."

Emily brightened. "He is?"

"Yes." And Serena couldn't stop thinking about his words Friday night. If she continued to push God away, would the wall around her become insurmountable? Wasn't her real impediment an inability to forgive herself? Didn't her daughters deserve a mom who was spiritually strong and could continue to guide them in the truth—especially now, with their father gone? She couldn't continue like this. It was selfish. Her family needed her. The questions had haunted her all day yesterday, and the guilt overwhelmed her. What was the real reason she had avoided God all these years?

"Mom." Emily laid a gentle hand on her arm to get her attention. "Are you okay?"

Serena looked down into her daughter's tender, trusting eyes. "I'll be fine."

⁊

When their taxi pulled into the church parking lot, Serena spotted Carson's car immediately, and she felt a familiar tingle of warmth.

He met her and Emily just inside the church doors and, to Serena's relief, led them to a seat near the back, where Serena would feel less conspicuous. In spite of the low profile, however, members spotted her immediately. Within minutes she was surrounded by old, dear friends, former members of her Sunday school class, and choir members. They welcomed her back to church, asked where she'd been, told her how much they missed her, and wished she would return home where she belonged.

She felt welcomed. She felt overwhelmed and deeply touched. She felt more than that. She felt the hand of God reaching out to her, drawing her, and reassuring her. For the first time, she dared to open her heart to what He was saying. Could He really want her? After all she had done, after all the running and avoiding, could He still truly want to be a part of her life?

During a lull in the visits, Carson leaned over and whispered in her ear. "It does get to you, doesn't it?"

She glanced at him briefly. "Yes."

"Were you surprised by the welcome?"

She glanced around her old church, at the stained glass windows, the beautiful floral decoration at the altar, and the comfortable padded pews. What mattered to her now, however, was the familiar faces of old friends who had cared enough to call her for months after Jennings died, urging her to return, and loving her through the grief.

"Serena?" Carson said. "Surprised?"

"No. Now that I think about it, I'm not surprised. I'm relieved. Nothing has changed."

"This is part of your family. They want you back."

Serena looked up at him questioningly, but before she could reply, the pastor came by to welcome them. Soon after he left, the singing began. Serena discovered that Carson had a beautiful bass voice, but the fact only registered superficially. Her mind was busy with his remark. They wanted her back—but did she belong here? Did she belong to God? If she did, why didn't she feel close to Him? Why couldn't she talk to Him the way Blythe or the girls did? Or Carson? Carson's faith was so simple, yet foundational in everything he did.

Halfway through the third hymn, her voice faltered. Sudden awareness rushed in at her, like a discovery of hidden treasure. Memories came together in a single thread of truth that stunned her. She stopped singing and felt Carson glance at her with concern. She didn't look at him. Emily touched her arm, and she shook her head.

Throughout her life, she had not experienced the faith that Carson and her family shared because she didn't own it, herself. She'd borrowed her parents' godly rituals when she was growing up in that grim, cheerless household, but rules were enough for them. When she married Jennings, she'd adopted his enthusiasm for serving the church, but while she allowed his values to become her own, she had never taken them into her heart. With his death, her connection to the things of God had disappeared. She had never had that personal, one-on-one experience with Jesus Christ. She glanced at Carson, then away.

It didn't come as a surprise to her when the sermon that morning was about forgiveness. She often heard other people complain that they felt a particular sermon was directed at them, but this was the first time it had happened to her. She had no complaints. She listened hungrily to the pastor's words about God's forgiveness, never once feeling conspicuous or out of place; never giving it another thought as her soul drank in the words she had longed to hear for so many years. She'd heard it all before, but she had never felt they applied to her own life, never felt that God could forgive her until now. She bowed her head and said a silent prayer, repenting, releasing the burden she had held within her for so long, and the tremendous load of guilt slipped away.

When she stood with everyone for the invitation song, she felt hope rise in her heart—hope, and an intense desire to meet with the Savior she had so long rejected. She put her song book down and stepped toward the aisle, then hesitated and looked back at Carson. He watched her expectantly.

"Would you come with me to the altar?"

He nodded and replaced his hymnal, his eyes never leaving her face until she turned to walk ahead of him.

As they knelt at the front of the church, she felt God's love encompassing them both, and tears of happiness came to her eyes as words of praise sprang to her lips. "Thank You, God, for sending Your messenger to talk with me." She reached across and squeezed Carson's arm. "Thank You for giving me the peace I've rejected for so many years, and thank You for Your forgiveness. Although I don't deserve it, please give me Your gift of life. I want to be Yours."

The congregation continued to sing as Serena raised her head and looked at Carson through the lingering tears.

"Thank you," she whispered.

&

After the benediction, Emily rushed down to the front of the church and flung herself into Serena's arms, her face wet with tears. "Mom, you did it! You did it!" She kissed Serena on the cheek. "Jenny and I have been praying for you for so long!"

Fresh tears rose in Serena's throat as she thought of her daughters, Blythe, and Carson, all praying for her. Now their prayers, and hers, had been answered. Serena felt clean, spiritually refreshed, ready for that new beginning they had told Kirby about. All the old depression left her, and she felt nothing but praise for God. She had been blind to Him for so long and had just now received sight. It was a wonderful feeling.

A friend of Emily's asked her to spend the afternoon, and Carson requested that Serena allow him to take her home. It was time for that talk she had been dreading. Somehow, she didn't dread it quite so much now.

With growing certainty, Serena realized that, not only must she tell Carson about her past, but she must tell her family. It had been a secret for too long. She thought of Emily and Jenny, of their sweet, all-encompassing love for her. Nothing could change that. And Blythe was never one to pass judgment. Serena would wait until Blythe came home to tell them, but today she would tell Carson.

How would he react?

When he pulled into Serena's driveway and parked, she reached across and touched his arm hesitantly. "Would you take a walk with me? We have some talking to do."

He held her gaze, unsmiling. "Sounds serious."

She opened her own door quickly and got out. She knew she couldn't expect to feel perfect peace at a time like this, not when Carson's reaction could affect her so much; but she had expected to be a little calmer, hadn't thought she would have so much trouble breathing. This mattered so much. She reached the end of the driveway and turned onto the sidewalk in front of the house, her strides lengthening.

"Hey, want to wait for me?" Carson called from behind her.

She slowed her steps and allowed him to catch up. "Sorry. There's something I should have told you sooner, something I've been ashamed for you to know. It's why I've been a little hesitant about. . .about our relationship."

"A little?"

She smiled. "Okay, very resistant."

"And I've told you more than once that nothing can change my heart."

"Yes, but you have no idea. . ." She turned to him and stopped.

"Don't you think it's time?" he asked softly.

"Yes." She turned away and stepped along the sidewalk once more. "Next Friday would have been my daughter's birthday. She would have been twenty years old now. . .if she were alive. If I hadn't aborted her." The words scattered into the air, and she caught her breath, suddenly wishing she could recall them.

Serena couldn't look at Carson. "I was seventeen at the time. There were complications during the procedure, which is why I can't have children." She kept walking. "It's the one thing I couldn't bring myself to forgive and I couldn't allow God to forgive. The pain was too great, and I think I wanted to suffer. I felt I deserved it. I felt that the suffering would take away some of the intense guilt I felt I couldn't live with. Jennings never knew. I kept that from him for so many years, and the guilt compounded, because I knew it was my fault, my choice, that also kept him from having children of his own."

Carson caught her arm and pulled her around to face him. His dark eyes held compassion. "That's what you've kept secret all these years? How could you have worked with all those women and shown such openness and empathy with

Kirby when you couldn't find it in your heart to forgive yourself? The abortion must have been horrible for you."

"It was. I know I'll still have to struggle to continue to forgive myself. I'll live with it always. I'll never forget the loss." She turned to walk back toward the house, and Carson fell into step beside her.

"Why have you waited to tell me this? Surely you didn't think I would hold it against you. Who am I to blame you when God casts no blame?"

She couldn't answer.

"I love you, Serena. Nothing has changed except that I love you more all the time. I love your family. I want to marry you."

Serena's chest swelled with overwhelming happiness and gratitude, but she had to cover everything. "I could never have your children. You've never had children of your own."

"I'm not looking for someone to have children for me. You have two wonderful girls already, and if we decided to adopt, we could. You're the one I want to share my life with."

She slowed and stopped at her porch steps, then turned to look up into his face. He was telling her the simple truth. He wanted her as she was. She smiled and laid her hand against the side of his face. "You really want to marry me?" She didn't deserve the joy of looking into his eyes and seeing the adoration he had for her.

"I want to marry you, Serena," he said softly. "I've told you before, I'm lonely, and it's all your fault. I was settled and satisfied until you came into my life, then I realized how wonderful life can be with someone who is caring and giving and fascinating. You are so much more than I ever dreamed possible. Please marry me."

She leaned into the warm, embracing strength of his arms. "Name the time and the place, Carson Tanner. I'll be there."

eighteen

The hot Sunday afternoon sun dropped below a tree-shrouded horizon, leaving heat in its wake. Dusk fell as two men in dark clothing strode with careful casualness down the alley behind the strip of older buildings where Alternative was nestled. Both men were empty-handed. The taller, heavier man wore a light nylon jacket, zipped up to the neck, undoubtedly uncomfortable in the lingering humidity. He frowned at his smaller companion. "You sure about this?"

"Doesn't it make sense? Why go all the way to Columbia when we can gouge out the cancer in our own city? This is a silent cancer. Nobody even suspects what goes on here. But I know."

"Have you been inside the clinic?"

"Yes, I have. I went inside one day when the volunteer was talking with a girl in the back."

"Well? Did you see anything interesting?"

"Not then, but don't forget I talked to that Acuff woman, and she was really suspicious about the place."

"Yeah, but you, yourself, said the woman was upset because her daughter went to live with Dr. Van Buren."

"Sure she was, but I was still curious. What would you have been thinking when you saw Van Buren talking to Wells at the school?" He turned to his companion and waited for a reply, as if the answer had better be good.

"They could have been arguing."

"Or setting up an appointment to check out her clinic for a future death site. Get a clue, Freeman! That's your problem, you don't see trouble until it's smashing you in the face!" His voice rose with increased fervor. "And that monster had the guts to openly come right to this clinic to see her. He's spitting in our faces, don't you see that? He won't be killing babies on this street."

"Not at this address, anyway."

"He was here for a long time, too, and he didn't hang around in the front. They took him to one of those back rooms." Edward stopped at the back door of the clinic. "She's a hypocrite!" His anger was palpable and growing again. "I wonder how many girls have their abortions right here in this place."

Freeman nodded in agreement, catching Edward's excitement. "Yeah, I wonder."

Edward tried the door handle and found it locked, as he had known it would be. "There's no one here to get hurt." He reached into his pocket and pulled out a thin strip of metal.

Freeman stared at it in surprise.

"I didn't just loaf outside this place for two weeks," Edward said. "I learned a little about jimmying locks."

The tool didn't work as efficiently as it could have, so it took Edward five agonizingly long minutes to jiggle it open and swing back the door. "After you."

Freeman hesitated and peered inside. "Dark in there. Can I turn on a light?"

"Maybe you'd better use your flashlight. Never know who might drive past out front."

Freeman did what Edward suggested and eased through the door.

❧

"Uh-oh, I almost forgot." Jenny pressed the brake of the van and turned onto High Street. "We were supposed to drop these things off at the clinic. It's a good thing we've got the van. I can't believe how generous those people are at Memorial."

Kirby looked at her watch. "We're kind of late, aren't we? Won't Serena be worried? Why don't we call?"

"Okay, but we can do it from the clinic. Mom doesn't like me talking on the cell phone when I'm driving. This will only take a few minutes, then we can get on home. A couple of people are supposed to drop by the clinic first thing in the morning, and these things should help. Mom will understand when I tell her why we're late."

Kirby's blue eyes widened. "You're going to tell her Danny came to the cabin?"

"Why shouldn't I? Nothing happened."

"And she'll believe that?"

"Sure she will. Why not?"

"My mom never would."

Jenny hesitated, stopping at a light. "Mom knows I don't lie to her," she said quietly. She didn't look at Kirby, but she could feel the other girl's sudden tension.

"I do," Kirby said quietly. "It's kind of a habit I got into a long time ago. Now it's just natural. Mother wouldn't believe me if I told the truth, anyway."

"Why don't you try it and see what happens? You didn't do anything this weekend you would have to lie about."

"No, but if I told her we went on that boat ride with those two guys—"

"Friends from church."

"That wouldn't matter to her. She'd think the worst."

They pulled up to the curb right in front of Alternative. Jenny switched off the engine and pulled her keys from the ignition. She opened her door, glancing behind the van to make sure no traffic was coming.

"Want me to help carry?" Kirby asked.

"I can get these boxes. Maybe you shouldn't be lifting heavy stuff. Besides, if you stay here with Rascal, he won't bark." Jenny glanced across the street, turned to slide the cargo door open, then spun back around to stare at Alternative's glass front. All was dark. But just for a half second she thought—

Rascal's sudden bark startled her.

"Jenny? What's wrong?" Kirby asked.

Jenny watched the building a moment longer, then shrugged and reached around for the box of clothes. "Nothing. I just thought I saw a light in the clinic, but it was probably just a reflection from a passing car." She glanced up and down the street, which was empty of traffic for the moment. The sky, totally dark now, loomed closely overhead without moon or stars to break its heaviness. Kirby had mentioned a cloud bank behind them on their way up from the lake.

Jenny shivered, though she wasn't cold. Even in Jefferson City, Missouri, downtown didn't feel like a safe place to be at night. She would hurry and drop off the supplies and leave. She warned Rascal to stay put and hefted the box to her hip, glad of the lights spaced closely together along the sidewalks. In spite of her command, Rascal leaped from the van and raced to her side, brushing so closely to her leg, he nearly tripped her. Having accompanied Serena often when she came down to lock up, he was familiar with the clinic. Tonight, though, he hesitated before he reached the front door. His front legs stiffened. Golden hairs stood up at the nape of his neck, and he growled.

Jenny stopped, heartbeats quickening. Then she shook her head in exasperation. "Silly! Are you trying to scare the life out of me? Stop fooling around!"

She set her box on the sidewalk and held her key ring up to the light.

Rascal barked.

Jenny ignored him, found the key, and stuck it into the lock.

Rascal barked again.

"Stop it I said! You're not even supposed to—"

Jenny glanced up and saw—this time she was certain—a flash of light at the opening that led into the conference room.

"Jenny!" Kirby called. "What's taking you so long? Your

mom is going to be really worried. What's wrong? You should have called her as soon as we got here. Tell me how to use this phone, and—"

Jenny whirled around, grabbed the dog, and bolted for the van, leaving the clothes sitting on the sidewalk.

"What is it? Are you crazy?" Kirby exclaimed. "Somebody'll steal that before morning!"

Jenny shoved Rascal into the back, closed the cargo door, and jumped in the front seat, her face pale, her heart pounding her rib cage.

"Somebody's in there!" She pressed the button that locked all the doors, then glanced at Kirby's disbelieving expression. "I'm not kidding! I saw a light, like a flashlight. Rascal saw it, too. Didn't you hear him barking?"

Kirby's eyes grew larger. Her face drained of color. "Let's get out of here!"

Jenny started the engine, put the van in gear, then hesitated. "We can't."

"What? What do you mean we can't? If there's some goon in there, we can't just sit out here and wait for him to come and get us!"

"No, but we can't drive all the way home and leave him there to burglarize the place or vandalize it. We've got to call the police. And Mom." She drove the van a short way down the street, pulled the cell phone from the glove compartment of the van, and dialed.

※

For at least the tenth time tonight, Serena turned from the window that overlooked the street. Carson had gone home hours ago, Emily was spending the night with a friend, and Serena had been unable to settle to the work she brought home from the office.

Where were Jenny and Kirby? They should have been home long before dark. Suppose something had happened to them?

Serena had no way to get to them quickly. But what could happen? Jenny wasn't likely to do anything stupid. She was a good driver. The van had all new tires on it and it was in peak running condition. That was another thing Blythe took care—

The telephone rang beside her. She jumped and grabbed it. "Hello?"

"Mom, this is Jenny. I'm down at Alternative, and something's going on. I went to deliver these baby things, and I saw a light flickering inside."

The cold chill of dread raced up Serena's spine. "And you're still there? Jenny, get out of there now!"

"I called the police, and they're already on their way. The silent alarm went off. Everything's all right, Mom, really. It's under control."

"And I know you, Jenny Van Buren. You'll try to play hero. Come home."

There was a pause, then Jenny said, "Can't we just lock the doors and sit tight until the police get here?"

Serena's heart pounded. She needed to get down there, and Carson could get here faster than Jenny could. "Okay, fine. I'll call and see if Carson will bring me down there, but you sit tight and wait for the police."

"Okay, Mom."

"And lock the van doors."

"They're locked."

"Good girl. I'll be there as soon as I can. I love you, Honey." She disconnected and dialed Carson's number.

❧

Edward peered over Freeman's shoulder at the dynamite that stuck out of a freshly drilled hole in the wall. "Why is this taking so long?"

"You want to destroy the supports, don't you? We've got to do it just right."

"But inside the walls? Is it necessary?"

"Yes. Are you sure the fire won't spread to other buildings?"

"Shouldn't—they're bricked. Besides, the fire department will get here in a hurry after the explosion."

"Explosions." Freeman straightened. "There should be three, if I've done it right."

"How much time will we have to get out of here?"

"How much do you want?"

"Ten minutes should do it."

"Go on to the door and I'll meet you there."

Edward didn't use his flashlight to find his way. No sense in taking chances this close to their objective. He crept along the night-blackened hall with his hands out like huge antennae. He reached the door and pulled it open to a blare of blinding light, the sharp, metallic clack of a safety being released, and the resonant voice of a policeman advising him that he was under arrest. In a state of shock, he heard his Miranda rights as he laced his hands behind his head.

They repeated the procedure a moment later when Freeman stepped out.

≈

Jenny caught her breath and grasped Kirby's arm, scrambling back into the shadows behind the police car. "It's him! It's that Edward guy who wrote those fliers!"

"What was he doing in the clinic?"

"I don't know, but I'm going to find out."

"The police won't let you in right now, will they?"

"Maybe not, but I can try. Let's go around to the front."

Reluctantly, Kirby followed Jenny through the darkness, glancing behind them frequently at the flashing lights of the police car. They were halfway around when they heard shouts from the alley. Seconds later two more policemen ran around from the front with their guns out.

"It's okay, we got him," one of the officers announced. "He thought he could outrun us. Better keep an eye on these two."

"Come on," Jenny whispered, leading the way to the front. "They've got them under control, and now's a good time to try to get inside."

"But Serena will be here any time. Can't we wait?"

Jenny stuck the key in the lock and turned. "That's why I want to check. Don't you realize how upset Mom will be if they've vandalized the place? Besides, what are you worried about? The police are here. We're perfectly safe." She picked up the box she had left on the sidewalk earlier and carried it through the door with her.

Kirby hesitated, watching Jenny switch on the lights. A policeman stepped into the main room from the back. Of course Jenny was right. It was safe. She was always careful, and the worst that could happen would be—

"Hey!" someone called from behind them. "Who are you, what are you doing in there? Get out—"

The ground lurched beneath Kirby's feet. A flash of light burned her vision. One millisecond later an explosion detonated in her ears. She staggered backward from the shock as the front windows shattered out onto the street.

A high-pitched wail followed the explosion, unrelenting, until Kirby realized it was her own screams. The scream formed a word: "Jenny!"

ಎ

Serena and Carson heard the explosion two blocks from the clinic. They saw the windows shatter, saw the lights go out. Figures bobbed and swayed, running through the darkness. Carson gunned the car through a stoplight.

Serena saw Kirby's slender, blond-haired form stumbling over the curb.

"No! Kirby, no!" Serena cried.

Carson honked the horn, and they screeched to a stop behind the van. They both jumped from the car in time for another explosion. And another.

"Serena!" Kirby shouted, running to them, choking on the black smoke that billowed into the street. "Jenny's in there! She went into the clinic!"

The words sent a shock wave through Serena. "Jenny," she whispered. "No." She stared through the shattered glass of the front window and bolted suddenly toward the front door. "Jenny!"

Carson grabbed her and dragged her backward. "Serena."

She fought his grip. "She's in there! What if there's another—"

Carson wrapped his arms around her struggling form. "You can't risk it right now. Look, the police are coming." He drew her more tightly still. "Serena, stop. You have to hold on for a minute."

She turned to him, met the deep fear in his eyes that matched her own. She grasped the front of his shirt, as if her grip would keep her steady, keep her from losing control. "Carson, we've got to get to her!"

"I know. We will."

Already, they heard sirens in the distance. A uniformed officer came running toward them from the end of the block, gesturing for them to move back.

Serena struggled once more in Carson's firm grip, and he released her. She ran toward the policeman. "My daughter was in there! Please, you've got to help us. She ran into the building just before the explosion, and—"

"Are you Serena Van Buren?" the officer demanded.

"Yes. My daughter—"

"Jenny? Is that your daughter?"

She caught her breath and looked more closely at him. "Jenny, yes! Is she—"

"We've called an ambulance, ma'am. She was in the rear hallway when the first explosion detonated at the front of the building. Two of my men had just apprehended her for—"

"But how badly is she hurt? Take me to her."

"She says she's fine, ma'am, we just want to take—"

"She says she's fine?" Sudden relief weakened Serena's legs. She stumbled, and Carson put his arm around her shoulders for support.

"She didn't even want us to call an ambulance. I imagine it will just be a treat-and-release, but we didn't want to take any chances. I think your daughter will be okay."

᠔᠕

Two hours later, Serena opened her front door to find Carol and Hal Acuff standing on the porch, their faces tense. "Dr. Van Buren, thanks for calling us," Hal said. "We saw the news report on TV, but we didn't realize Kirby was involved until you told us. Is she here? Can we see her?"

"Of course, come on in. We're all still sitting around in shock." Serena stepped back and waited for them to enter.

Carol paused in front of her and searched her eyes. "I'm sorry about the explosion." Her voice was soft, and she was more subdued than Serena had ever seen her. She reached out and touched Serena's arm. "Are you going to be okay?"

"Now that I know Jenny and Kirby are safe. That's all that really matters. It looks like we'll have to have our meetings here for awhile, or at my office downtown."

"The clinic was destroyed?"

"Totally." Serena heard her own voice wobble. She swallowed. "We'll rebuild."

Carol squeezed her arm. "Good." She paused, glanced toward her husband, then looked back at Serena. "We've done a lot of talking these past few days, Serena. And I've done a lot of thinking. I've had to. I can't stand the thought of losing my daughter because of my own stubbornness."

Hal stepped up beside her and laid a hand on his wife's shoulder. "What we're trying to say is that we'll help Kirby through this pregnancy. We want to do whatever it takes to make this family work."

"Tonight cinched it for us," Carol said. "I just kept asking myself, 'What if Kirby had been in that building? What if we'd lost her?' I couldn't stand the thought." Her eyes filled with tears. "I'm still struggling with the idea of being a grandmother before I'm forty, but I've got some time to get ready for that."

"Mom? Dad?" came a timid, wavering voice from the hallway, and the three of them turned to find Kirby standing there, her blue eyes—so much like her mother's—wide and questioning.

"Kirby." Carol's face crumpled, and the accumulation of tears trickled down her cheeks. "Oh, Baby, we're so glad you're safe." She reached for her daughter, and Kirby rushed into her arms. Hal put his arms around both of them, and Serena quietly left them alone. They had a long way to go, a lot of healing to do, but she intended to see they got all of the help they needed.

She stepped into the family room and saw Carson sprawled out on the carpet between Jenny and Emily, laughing at Rascal's attempt to reach a cookie from the end table. Carson caught sight of Serena, and the laughter in his eyes deepened to something more powerful, filled with joy. He winked and beckoned her to join them.

Serena had never felt more complete.

*E*ight lives are forever altered by the events of one day. Whether they were on the plane or share a more distant connection, these four young couples find a dark mystery haunting their budding romances. Waiting for God to work everything out could be their biggest challenge yet.

Locked by the past, CJ and Brad have only *A Wing and a Prayer* left to look toward the future. *Wings Like Eagles* are needed to pull Christy and Curt out of the grips of a tangled web. Cheryl and Erik have an unlikely chance to start over on the *Wings of the Dawn*. And, Debbie and Nathan receive *A Gift of Wings*, allowing forgiveness and healing to take place.

The Denver air is filled with intrigue and romance in these three complete novels and one bonus novella, all by best-selling author Tracie Peterson.

paperback, 464 pages, 5 ³⁄₁₆" x 8"

♥ ♥ ♥ ♥ ♥ ♥ ♥ ❤ ♥ ♥ ♥ ♥ ♥ ♥ ♥

♥ ♥ ♥ ♥ ♥ ♥ ♥ ❤ ♥ ♥ ♥ ♥ ♥ ♥ ♥

A Letter To Our Readers

Dear Reader:

In order that we might better contribute to your reading enjoyment, we would appreciate your taking a few minutes to respond to the following questions. We welcome your comments and read each form and letter we receive. When completed, please return to the following:

Rebecca Germany, Fiction Editor
Heartsong Presents
PO Box 719
Uhrichsville, Ohio 44683

1. Did you enjoy reading *A Living Soul?*
   ☐ Very much. I would like to see more books
      by this author!
   ☐ Moderately
      I would have enjoyed it more if _____
      _____
      _____

2. Are you a member of **Heartsong Presents**? Yes ☐ No ☐
   If no, where did you purchase this book? _____
   _____

3. How would you rate, on a scale from 1 (poor) to 5 (superior),
   the cover design? _____

4. On a scale from 1 (poor) to 10 (superior), please rate the
   following elements.

   _____ Heroine   _____ Plot

   _____ Hero   _____ Inspirational theme

   _____ Setting   _____ Secondary characters

5. These characters were special because_____

_____

_____

6. How has this book inspired your life?_____

_____

_____

7. What settings would you like to see covered in future
   Heartsong Presents books?_____

_____

_____

8. What are some inspirational themes you would like to see
   treated in future books?_____

_____

_____

9. Would you be interested in reading other **Heartsong
   Presents** titles?   Yes ❑   No ❑

10. Please check your age range:
    ❑ Under 18   ❑ 18-24   ❑ 25-34
    ❑ 35-45   ❑ 46-55   ❑ Over 55

11. How many hours per week do you read?_____

Name _____

Occupation _____

Address _____

City _____ State _____ Zip _____

Shake out the confetti and celebrate another year full of sweet promise and true blessings. It is the best time of the year to set new goals. Make it your first goal to snuggle back into a cozy chair and relish these four narratives of love.

Rejoice in the life-changing transformation of a young woman in *Remaking Meredith* by Carol Cox. Laugh (and cry) through *Beginnings*, Peggy Darty's story of two lonely adults who are confined to the hospital over the holiday season. Then discover how goal setting brings a church singles' class together and sparks the flame of love in *Never Say Never* by Yvonne Lehman. Finally, in *Letters to Timothy*, see how author Pamela Kaye Tracy unites five needy people with one pen pal letter.

Resolve to rediscover the glory of love with these four timeless stories.

paperback, 352 pages, 5 ³⁄₁₆" x 8"

♥ ♥ ♥ ♥ ♥ ♥ ♥ ❤ ♥ ♥ ♥ ♥ ♥ ♥ ♥

♥ ♥ ♥ ♥ ♥ ♥ ♥ ❤ ♥ ♥ ♥ ♥ ♥ ♥ ♥

Hearts♥ng Presents
Love Stories Are Rated G!

That's for godly, gratifying, and of course, great! If you love a thrilling love story, but don't appreciate the sordidness of some popular paperback romances, **Heartsong Presents** is for you. In fact, **Heartsong Presents** is the *only inspirational romance book club* featuring love stories where Christian faith is the primary ingredient in a marriage relationship.

Sign up today to receive your first set of four, never before published Christian romances. Send no money now; you will receive a bill with the first shipment. You may cancel at any time without obligation, and if you aren't completely satisfied with any selection, you may return the books for an immediate refund.

Imagine. . .four new romances every four weeks—two historical, two contemporary—with men and women like you who long to meet the one God has chosen as the love of their lives. . . all for the low price of $9.97 postpaid.

To join, simply complete the coupon below and mail to the address provided. **Heartsong Presents** romances are rated G for another reason: They'll arrive *Godspeed!*